OUTCAST

As if from far away, Molly heard herself say, "I could come with you."

Buzz gaped at her, astonished. "No! I couldn't ask you to run away—no."

Molly shook her head, trying to dispel the fog of pain and confusion. What was she saying? Was she totally crazy?

But instead of rejection, here was an offer of something more, something better. And it was coming from someone who said he wanted her. She hadn't heard much of that lately. "There's nothing to keep me here," she said, rubbing her tired eyes with the heel of her hand.

Faces and voices swam into Molly's imagination—angry faces, harsh voices accusing her of tormenting Regina Morrow and driving her to her death. How dare they treat her that way! Well, she would show them. She would show them what they'd get for treating her so badly.

A sob welled up in her throat. "Those— those pigs," she said angrily. I can't think of anything bad enough to call them! But they'll see. I'll show them. I'm going with you, Buzz. They'll be sorry. All of them."

Bantam Books in the Sweet Valley High Series
Ask your bookseller for the books you have missed

SWEET VALLEY HIGH

OUTCAST

Written by
Kate William

Created by
FRANCINE PASCAL

BANTAM BOOKS
TORONTO · NEW YORK · LONDON · SYDNEY · AUCKLAND

RL 6, IL age 12 and up

OUTCAST
A Bantam Book / November 1987

Sweet Valley High is a registered trademark of Francine Pascal.

Conceived by Francine Pascal

Produced by Cloverdale Press, Inc.
133 Fifth Avenue, New York, NY 10003

Cover art by James Mathewuse

ISBN 0-553-26866-X

Published simultaneously in the United States and Canada

PRINTED IN THE UNITED STATES OF AMERICA

O   0 9 8 7 6 5 4 3 2 1

OUTCAST

One

Elizabeth Wakefield wiped her eyes with a tissue; her hand was trembling with emotion. She and her boyfriend, Jeffrey French, moved slowly toward the door of the auditorium of Sweet Valley High as the crowd filed out. All around her were the sounds of muffled crying—heart-wrenching tears of grief like the ones Elizabeth had been shedding since the night her friend Regina Morrow had died.

Nicholas Morrow, Regina's brother, had asked her to speak at the service. She had managed not to cry as she spoke. But as soon as she was offstage, she had begun crying again. Now, her throat ached, and her chin quivered uncontrollably as a sob welled up to the surface again.

Pressing her fist against her mouth, Elizabeth looked up into Jeffrey's deep green eyes. He had been crying, too.

For a moment neither of them spoke: the pain of Regina's tragic death went too deep for words. Then Jeffrey tenderly brushed a lock of honey-gold hair from Elizabeth's forehead and gave her a faint, pained smile. "I love you so much, Liz," he whispered. "If anything ever—"

"Shhh." Elizabeth put a finger to his lips and shook her head. "Don't even think about it!" she pleaded. She drew a shaky breath. "I have to go find Bruce and Amy," she said, fighting for control. "It's important."

Jeffrey nodded. "I'll be waiting for you."

As they walked outside into the blinding sunshine, Elizabeth caught sight of Bruce Patman and Amy Sutton, who were standing somewhat apart from the crowd. Until recently, Bruce and Regina had been a steady couple. But then things had changed: Bruce and Amy started working together on a project that threw them together constantly, and they began secretly dating. When Regina found out about it she was devastated, and as an act of defiance, she began hanging out with a wild bunch of kids. She accused her old friends of betraying her by not telling her about Amy and Bruce, and she tried to start over again without them. And now . . .

2

Now Regina was dead. Her feelings of rejection and betrayal had driven her down a fatal road. When her new friend Justin Belson had invited her to a party with a group of kids known to use drugs, she said yes. It was a big mistake. To prove that she wasn't an outsider, Regina had agreed to try some cocaine. She had had an extremely rare reaction to the drug. Her heartbeat had accelerated, bringing on sudden cardiac failure. A heart murmur she had had since birth had aggravated the reaction. She had fallen into a coma and never woke up again.

"Bruce? Amy?" Elizabeth spoke softly, and they turned to face her. There was a look of despair on Bruce's handsome face, and his jaw was tightly clenched. Amy's cheeks were streaked with tears, but she held Bruce's hand defiantly.

Elizabeth took a deep breath. "I just wanted you to know that Regina—Regina understood," she began, her voice cracking from emotion. "She wrote me a letter the night she—that night—and said she didn't hold—anything against you, so—so—"

Bruce pressed his lips together so hard the edges turned white, and tears welled up in his eyes. Elizabeth's heart ached to see him in such pain, and she put one hand on his arm as tears spilled down her own cheeks.

"Thanks, Liz," he choked out. He turned away quickly.

Amy gave Elizabeth a long, searching look. "Is that true?" she whispered. Long ago, Amy and Elizabeth had been best friends. Then the Suttons had moved to Connecticut, and Elizabeth had thought her childhood friend was gone forever. Recently, though, the Suttons had moved back to Sweet Valley, and Elizabeth had been ecstatic at the thought of renewing their old ties. But Amy had changed over the years into a frivolous, boy-crazy girl, and it was impossible to rekindle their friendship. Now, for the first time since Amy's return, Elizabeth felt as if they were looking straight into each other's hearts.

Elizabeth met Amy's worried gaze and nodded slowly, and Amy let out a long, drawn-out sigh of relief and sadness. Neither of them could speak, and finally Elizabeth just walked away.

She rejoined Jeffrey underneath a tree on the lawn. "Let's go home," she said wearily.

Putting his arm around her shoulders, Jeffrey gave her a comforting squeeze. Then they left Sweet Valley High and headed for Elizabeth's house.

The familiar scenery of their pretty California

town flashed by as they drove away from the school. Elizabeth drew comfort from the everyday solidness of the trees, the houses, and the sun shining above. She turned to Jeffrey and shook her head in amazement.

"You know, this all happened so quickly, I almost can't take it in."

He nodded ruefully. "I know what you mean. It's hard to believe that just over a week ago, Regina was still—alive."

"What I really wonder about is why she went to that party in the first place," Elizabeth continued, frowning. "I mean, I know she was spending time with Justin, but what would she want to go to Molly Hecht's party for? They're all pretty messed-up kids in that group. She knew that. I just . . ." Her voice trailed off, and she swallowed hard. None of it made any sense to her. How could pretty, confident Regina have let anyone talk her into using drugs? She just didn't seem like the type to get pressured into doing something, or to say to herself, "Why not? Just this once." Elizabeth couldn't imagine how it ever could have happened.

"Here we are," Jeffrey said quietly. The car rolled to a stop in front of a big split-level house. Ahead of them, parked by the sidewalk, were a brown Ford LTD and an old yellow Volkswagen.

Elizabeth squared her shoulders. "Looks like

5

my whole family is home," she observed, trying to make her voice sound normal. "They all knew about today's memorial service."

"Hey." Jeffrey turned her face to his and looked steadily into her eyes. His own eyes were filled with compassion and love. "Are you going to be OK?" he asked gently.

Before she could speak, a red Fiat convertible roared to a stop behind them. As she glanced over her shoulder, Elizabeth sighed. She looked back at Jeffrey and touched his cheek softly. "Yeah. I'll be fine." They kissed tenderly, and then Elizabeth stepped out of the car and watched as Jeffrey drove away.

Then she turned to face the one person who knew better than anyone else how she felt: her identical twin, Jessica. The girl facing Elizabeth was her mirror image: the same sun-streaked blond hair, the same dimpled left cheek, the same slim, five-foot, six-inch figure, the same healthy California tan.

The similarity only went as deep as the tan, however, because Elizabeth and Jessica had wildly different personalities. Jessica—the younger twin by four minutes—lived in a helter-skelter fashion, changing her wardrobe and her boyfriends with breathtaking speed. More responsible and thoughtful, Elizabeth preferred quiet times with her close friends to wild parties. And she often felt like pulling her hair out over her twin's exploits.

But even though in many ways the two girls were very different, the bond they shared as identical twins went deeper than anything else. Their eyes locked, and then they rushed into each other's arms.

"Oh, Lizzie!" Jessica wailed. "I wish it were just a bad dream."

"Me, too, Jess. Me, too."

For a moment Elizabeth stroked Jessica's hair. Jessica had never been a great friend of Regina's, but her grief was just as real as Elizabeth's. Always tempestuous, always in high gear, Jessica Wakefield felt everything with an intensity that Elizabeth found exhausting.

But in the end the twins always found more comfort in each other than in anyone else. With their arms around each other's shoulders, they walked up to the house.

Steven, the twins' older brother, opened the front door and nodded over his shoulder. "We're all in the kitchen," he said quietly. "Mom and Dad thought we should have a family conference."

Elizabeth gave her older brother a faint smile. "You didn't have to come home from college for us, Steve."

"Forget it." He cleared his throat gruffly as

7

he led the way inside. "I know how you must feel."

It hadn't been that long ago that eighteen-year-old Steven Wakefield had watched his girlfriend, Tricia Martin, die of leukemia. His grief had been deep and long lasting, and his family had stood by him all the way. Elizabeth knew he was remembering that ordeal now, and that he wanted to do something for his sisters because they had lost a friend, too.

The girls followed their brother into the cheerful, Spanish-tiled kitchen. At the table sat Ned and Alice Wakefield, their faces filled with sympathy and understanding as they welcomed their daughters. Blond, pretty, and slim, Mrs. Wakefield was sometimes mistaken for the twins' older sister. But at the moment she was all maternal concern. She rose and came forward, her hands outstretched.

"Hi, girls," she said, taking them each by the hand. She looked intently into Jessica's eyes and then switched her gaze to Elizabeth.

As her eyes met her mother's vivid blue eyes, Elizabeth felt some of the bitter sadness lighten in her heart, as though her mother were helping to share the heavy burden. She smiled, suddenly very grateful and glad that her parents were there when she needed them.

"Let's sit down, all right?" Mrs. Wakefield

pulled two chairs out from the table and sat back down as her daughters took their seats. Elizabeth felt a wet touch on her hand. She smiled down tenderly at Prince Albert, the twins' Labrador retriever. Gazing earnestly into her eyes, he pressed against her leg as though sensing her unhappiness. She fondled his silky ears, grateful for his silent support.

"I thought we should talk about what happened," began Mr. Wakefield, who approached many family problems with the same methodical care he approached legal problems. He ran a hand through his dark, wavy hair and sighed. "Your mother and I want you to know—and you, too, Steve," he added with a nod in his son's direction, "that if there's ever anything that makes you feel as though drugs are the only answer—"

"Just stop and think for a minute," Mrs. Wakefield continued, leaning forward to rest her elbows on the table. "And then come to us. There's nothing you can't confide in us—nothing we wouldn't do *everything* possible to help you cope with."

Elizabeth stared at the sugar bowl, lost in thought. It hurt deeply that Regina hadn't felt able to confide in her. There had been a time when Regina told Elizabeth all her hopes and dreams. But when Regina had found out that

9

Elizabeth knew about Bruce and Amy and hadn't told her, Regina had thought of Elizabeth as a traitor.

"Regina may have felt betrayed and alone," Mrs. Wakefield went on, echoing Elizabeth's thoughts. "But even if she felt she couldn't talk to her parents, she did have other options."

"It can seem really tempting to turn to drugs to escape," Steven cut in, his eyes dark with emotion. "When Trish died, Betsy couldn't deal with it. She thought the only way to get over losing her sister was by numbing herself with drugs. But it isn't the answer. It never is."

Elizabeth shook her head. "But it was so unlike Regina. She was the last person I would have expected—"

"Well, she never would have done it if it hadn't been for Molly Hecht making her!" Jessica cried out suddenly, breaking her long silence. "It's all Molly's fault!"

Ned Wakefield shook his head. "No, Jess. It may have been her party, Molly may have given Regina a push, but it was Regina who held out her hand for the drugs. It was her decision."

"But Molly—"

Elizabeth reached for her sister's hand under the table and squeezed hard. She knew her parents and Steven were right—it *had* been Regina's decision. But another part of her agreed with Jessica. If it hadn't been for Molly Hecht throwing that party in the first place—and inviting her messed-up friends—maybe Regina would still be alive today.

Her eyes filled with tears again, and the sunny, plant-filled room blurred. No. No matter what, she would never be able to look at or think of Molly Hecht again without thinking of Regina and without feeling an aching emptiness.

She felt a pressure on her hand as Jessica squeezed back, and Elizabeth sent her sister a look of complete understanding.

"And another thing," their father went on. "I know you're probably asking yourselves: 'Why Regina? Why her?' Well, it could have been anyone—anyone at all who used cocaine or heroin or any other drug, or even liquor. She took a chance, and we all lost because of it."

The family sat in silence for a few moments, each one contemplating Mr. Wakefield's words.

"You know," Jessica began thoughtfully, "I know I wasn't always that nice to Regina—I mean, we weren't really ever close—but now that she's gone, I just wish there was something I could do."

"Oh, sweetheart, that's very generous of you." Alice Wakefield smiled tenderly at Jessica. "But just remembering what a sweet girl she was, and all the wonderful things she accomplished— that's the best way to remember her."

11

But Jessica shook her head. "No, Mom. I mean really *do* something. Something real. I—I want to make it up to Regina for not treating her better when I had the chance."

Elizabeth stared wide-eyed at her twin, surprised by the intensity in Jessica's voice. Although she hated to admit it, Elizabeth was slightly skeptical of Jessica's desire to do something in Regina's memory. There wasn't any lack of sincerity in her offer, but Jessica often got carried away with good intentions on the spur of the moment, then forgot them just as quickly. But maybe this time she really would do something.

Reaching across the table, Ned Wakefield touched Jessica's cheek. "You'll think of something, Jess. I know you will."

"But just remember, sweetheart," her mother put in gently. "Nothing will bring Regina back. We all have to remember that."

Nothing will bring Regina back. The words resounded in Elizabeth's head, and a picture formed in her mind. She had first seen Regina at a party, a laughing, beautiful, raven-haired girl who had just moved to Sweet Valley. Elizabeth hadn't been able to believe—no one had— that Regina was deaf; there was nothing handicapped about her, even though she had to watch intently to read lips when she was talking.

And then another image replaced that one: a triumphant Regina returning to school for the first time after a series of special treatments in Switzerland had given her normal hearing. No one had ever looked more full of joy and life than Regina Morrow did then.

"Excuse me," Elizabeth said quietly. She pushed herself up heavily and drew a shaky breath. "I think I'd like to be alone for a while. I'll be in my room."

She met her mother's eyes for a long, silent moment and read the concern in her gaze. "I'll be OK, Mom," she whispered, managing a slight smile. Then she walked steadily out the door and up the stairs to her room, Prince Albert padding loyally behind.

Carefully, slowly, as if it were a delicate, important task, Elizabeth closed her bedroom door and leaned against it. Then she began to feel as though all the life were draining from her body, and she dragged herself to a chair and sat down. If only this could be a bad dream. If only—

With tears welling up in her eyes again, Elizabeth took a letter from the top of her writing table and reread it.

I never admitted to myself that Bruce and I had drifted apart. He isn't to blame, either. Sometimes couples just change and grow apart. Seeing how jealous Molly has been has helped me to see that Amy wasn't really to blame at all. No one can really break up a couple in love.

I owe you an apology because I see now that you tried to act in my best interest. I've always admired you so much, Liz . . . I really am sorry, and hope our friendship will last forever.

The ink began to run in a few spots where Elizabeth's tears had fallen, and the words blurred on the page. She automatically refolded the letter, then rested her hands in her lap. Elizabeth stared sightlessly at the far wall and slowly shook her head. On the floor by the bed, Prince Albert raised his head and whined softly.

"Oh, Regina!" Elizabeth whispered. "I'm going to miss you so much!"

Two

Jessica set her lunch tray down and slid into a chair next to her friend, Lila Fowler. The cafeteria wasn't as noisy as usual that Monday. It seemed that some of the somberness of Friday's memorial service still hung in the air.

"Hi." Lila sighed. She took a sip of her diet soda and swirled the ice around in the cup as she stared at her salad.

Jessica echoed the sigh. "Hi. Here comes Cara."

The two girls watched silently as the third member of their trio, Cara Walker, pulled out a chair to join them. She met their eyes briefly and sat down.

For several minutes they simply ate their

lunches, not even bothering to talk. But Jessica's mind was still turning over and over the idea of doing something—she didn't know what—for Regina. Finally she leaned forward and crossed her arms on the table.

"Listen," she said, her expression serious. "You guys have to help me out. I want to do something to remember Regina by."

Cara raised one eyebrow. "Like what?"

With an impatient gesture, Jessica waved aside Cara's question. "That's just it. I don't know yet. That's why I need your help."

"Well, you're not giving us very much to go on," Lila drawled, pushing a gold bracelet farther up her arm. "Can you be a little more specific?"

Jessica pursed her lips. "Mmm. No. I just want to do something," she repeated.

"Great." Lila rolled her eyes and met Cara's puzzled gaze. "She wants to *do* something."

"OK, OK," Jessica said curtly. "Forget it. I'll think of something on my own."

They lapsed into silence again, and Jessica's gaze moved around the room as her mind worked on devising a plan. She tapped her foot nervously and bit her lip. After a few moments, her eyes came to rest on a solitary figure at the far end of the cafeteria, and her expression became indignant.

16

"There's Molly Hecht," she muttered darkly, glaring at the petite blonde. "I don't know how she can even show her face in this school."

Cara put down her sandwich and turned around in her chair to look. "I can't believe she's here!" she exclaimed. She shook her head. "The *nerve*."

"I really think she should be expelled," Lila added with a toss of her light brown hair.

Jessica nodded emphatically. "Really. Girls like her we can do without. I mean, I don't care what Mr. Cooper said about the Morrows not holding anyone responsible. It's Molly's fault, not Regina's."

Her friends nodded in agreement, and Jessica stormed on. "Anyone who gives that kind of a party and knows that derelict Buzz is definitely bad news." Everyone had heard about Buzz, the pusher who had supplied the drugs that killed Regina.

Cara shot another look over her shoulder at Molly. "Say, the police still haven't caught that guy, have they?"

"Are you kidding?" Lila snorted. "My father says the police in this town are worthless when it comes to that sort of thing."

Nodding slowly, Jessica absentmindedly took a bite of her pizza and pulled a long, gooey string of mozzarella cheese off the top. "I wonder where he is, though," she mused, licking her fingers. "Think he's still in Sweet Valley?"

Cara shuddered. "I hope not. The thought of a guy like that still hanging around here gives me the creeps."

The three contemplated Molly Hecht for a few moments. The girl's narrow, pinched face looked pale and drawn, and her feathery blond hair hung around her face like a curtain.

"Do you suppose *she* knows where he is?" Cara wondered aloud.

"Don't ask me!" Lila retorted. "I don't intend to ever speak to the girl."

Jessica frowned. "What about Justin Belson? He used to be a really good friend of hers before all this happened."

"But not anymore," Cara said. "I know he hasn't been hanging out with her and that druggy crowd lately."

"Well, he took Regina to Molly's party, didn't he?" Lila demanded.

Cara crossed her arms and cocked her head to one side. "Well, sure. But just the fact that he liked Regina is proof that he was reforming, isn't it?"

Lila's eyebrows went up skeptically.

"Listen," Jessica cut in, her voice authoritative. "I think it's pretty obvious that it's really all Molly's fault. Justin may have taken Regina to the party, but it was *Molly* who gave the party and *Molly* who invited Buzz. As far as I'm concerned, that means she as good as *made* Regina do the coke. She was insanely jealous because she still wanted Justin to like her, and she couldn't take it that he liked Regina."

Lila shrugged and took a mirror and lip gloss from her handbag. She applied a quick coat of gloss to her lips and studied her reflection for a moment. "Yeah, I guess you're right. Molly is the type of girl who'll never reform. She's bad news any way you look at her."

"You'd better believe I'm right!" Jessica said, glancing at Molly again. "And if she's a total outcast from now on, it's exactly what she deserves."

Sighing heavily, Justin Belson balled up his lunch bag and threw it into the trash. Shaking his head, he walked away and pushed through the cafeteria door. He needed air, needed to feel some release from the burden of pain and guilt he was feeling.

Outside the sun was blazing with its usual intensity. It seemed strange to him that the sun would still shine just as if nothing had happened. He threw himself down onto the grass under a tree and closed his eyes, wishing the whole world would simply disappear.

Flickering sunlight moved across his eyelids, creating bright, abstract patterns. If only he could turn everything into a series of meaningless patterns, maybe the pain would go away, he told himself. The old pain that had filled his life ever since his father had been killed senselessly in a robbery.

Justin sat up and looked around at the lush grass and vibrant sky. "Man, what a joke on me," he muttered with a bitter laugh. "Just when I thought life was treating me fairly again."

Just when he was building a wonderful friendship with Regina Morrow, a girl he had never *dreamed* he could reach, everything had come crashing down on him. All his happiness had been swept away in a single night. *And all because of Molly and her stupid jealousy*, he thought.

He glanced at the windows of the cafeteria behind him. *Well, maybe not totally because of Molly*, he admitted with reluctance. After all, he had been hanging around with that same wild crowd for a long time—ever since he'd lost his father. And he was the one who had brought Regina right into the middle of it.

At the party Molly and her friend Jan had done their best to make Regina feel uncomfortable and out of place. And it had worked. Regina had felt so awkward around that crowd that she had done the cocaine just to feel like part of the group. He knew the feeling.

"No more," he said through gritted teeth. "I'm not going to let them drag me down—let *this* drag me down. Not anymore."

He pounded the soft, moist grass with his clenched fist and shook his head. He would steer clear of them all from now on, he vowed. Even Molly—*especially* Molly. They may have been close once, he may have really loved her once, but now just the sight of her was an excruciating reminder of everything he had lost.

For his father's sake, and for Regina's sake, he would leave that whole crowd behind him. *A clean start,* he told himself. *Just try to pretend you never knew those people, never hung out with them, never liked any of them. Especially not Molly Hecht.*

"Justin?"

He froze. Scrambling to his feet, Justin turned and faced Molly. He swallowed hard.

Molly's thin face was pale, and her green eyes were filled with sorrow as she gazed up at him imploringly. "Justin, I—I saw you come out here, and I—"

Shaking his head, Justin began to back away.

"Justin, I need to talk to you. Please!" Her eyes pleaded with him as she took a step forward and put a hand on his arm.

He shook off her hand violently. "No," he said hoarsely. "No, I can't. I can't help you,

Molly." With one more look into her desperate eyes, Justin turned around and fled.

Molly stared after him, waves of guilt and loneliness washing over her. The friend she had always relied on had turned his back on her. They had been through so much together, she and Justin. Getting into drugs was the biggest mistake of her life, because that was what had started to drive him away. Now he was gone. Permanently. She had never felt so bad in her whole life.

And I deserve it. The certainty that Regina would still be alive if not for her was like a heavy stone in Molly's heart. She accepted the responsibility, regardless of what Mr. Cooper, the principal, and Regina's parents had said. After all, she *had* invited Regina to her party, she *had* goaded Regina into trying the cocaine, even though she could tell Regina didn't really want to. She admitted it.

But are you the only one to blame? a voice whispered in her heart. *What about Bruce and Amy? What about Justin and Buzz and Jan? And what about Regina herself? Am I the only one responsible? Am I the only one who's going to be a social outcast from now on?*

She stared down at the grass beneath her feet and shook her head. It was so unfair! Molly blinked rapidly, fighting back the tears that threatened to come. *I can't do this alone.*

I can't do this alone. The phrase echoed numbly in her head all afternoon as everywhere she went, she met accusing eyes. In her classes, in the hallways, no one spoke to her. People moved away as she passed, as though she were carrying some kind of deadly, contagious disease.

By the time the last bell rang, Molly felt as if she had been physically beaten. When everyone got up to leave the classroom at the end of the day, she stayed behind for a few minutes. There was no point in going out into the crowded hallway—she would only get more of the same thing. At last she poked her head out the door and was relieved to find the corridors empty. She headed for home automatically, hardly even aware of where she was. In the back of her mind, she knew that she had to be home on time because she was grounded indefinitely. But she walked slowly anyway, dragging her feet, hanging her head. It made no difference to her when she got home because when she did, she knew she would find no relief.

"You're late!" Molly's mother flung open the door and stood with her arms crossed as Molly dragged herself up the steps. "I thought we agreed you'd be here by three, and it's three-fifteen already."

Molly raised her eyes to her mother's and then dropped them. "Sorry," she mumbled.

"Sorry! Listen to me, young lady," her mother continued, following her inside. "When your father and I say be home on time, we mean it. Understand?"

Standing in the narrow hallway, Molly stared mutely at the floor, letting her mother's voice wash over her. It was just another wave of the same abuse she had been getting since Regina's death. Phrases such as "never forgive you" and "told you a hundred times" pounded against her ears. All Molly could do was concentrate on the pattern of boards running in straight lines along the floor.

It seemed ironic to her that even though her parents were divorced, they could still stick together against her. Her father had come down from San Francisco the week before, and he was as furious as her mother was.

"Is that Molly?" came her father's voice from the living room.

"Yes."

Heavy footsteps sounded on the hardwood floor, and Mr. Hecht's shoes appeared in Molly's line of vision. "Isn't it enough that you betrayed your mother's trust by throwing a party here alone, that you've been hanging around with the wrong kind of kids, let *alone* broke the law and did God knows what kind of drugs—"

"But that you can't even get back from *school* when we tell you to," Mrs. Hecht broke in, her voice becoming shrill.

Molly raised her head and met her parents' eyes. She shook her head, unable to speak. They stared back at her, their familiar faces now the faces of strangers.

"Well?" her father demanded. "What do you have to say?"

"I'm sorry," she choked out, suddenly short of breath. As she tried to fill her lungs, Molly felt her face grow hot, then cold, then hot again.

Mrs. Hecht frowned. "What is *wrong* with you?"

Molly shook her head. "Can't you—it wasn't my—I feel—"

"Whatever you feel, you should," Mr. Hecht stated firmly. "You're responsible for that lovely—"

"Dad! Please!" Molly looked desperately from her father to her mother and back again. "I know I did some terrible things, and I'll never be able to forget them for the rest of my life! But everyone's treating me like a murderer! Can't you give me a break?"

"A break? You want *us* to give *you* a break? You did this in *my* house, and you want a break?" her mother cried out incredulously. Angry tears began to spill down Mrs. Hecht's face. "I can't take this anymore! I can't!" She turned and ran from the hallway, sobbing.

Stony silence followed her departure. The ticking of a wall clock suddenly became audible.

Trying to compose herself, Molly spoke again, her voice quivering dangerously. "I'd like to transfer to another school, or even drop out. Or maybe I could come to San Francisco. . . ." Her words trailed off, her hope dying as she met her father's stern eyes.

He shook his head. "No, Molly. You're staying in Sweet Valley, and you're going to go to school every single day. You're going to face those kids and take it, and you're not staying home sick or dropping out or moving away. You're going to stay and take what's coming to you."

For another long moment, her father glared at her. Then he turned and strode back into the living room.

This can't be happening to me! Molly wanted to scream. *Why doesn't anyone understand?*

She gazed blankly at the walls around her. It was in this very house that everything had begun to go crazy. It all seemed so strange and unfamiliar to her now, as though it were an exact duplicate of her house but not really her house at all.

In her imagination she saw the front door

burst open and Nicholas Morrow stride in, angrily demanding to know where his sister was. She saw the ambulance arriving and taking Regina away, ghostly pale and hardly breathing. She remembered the terrible, ominous silence after someone pulled the plug on the stereo. And then the stunned, speechless faces of the people at the party as their eyes had riveted on her.

"Oh, God." Molly groaned now, and slumped to the floor. "I'm so sorry! I never meant for her to die!"

The one hope that Molly clung to was the thought that *someone* might understand what she was feeling. She also had a desperate need to make the people closest to Regina understand. People like Nicholas, and Elizabeth Wakefield. If only she could get through to them, maybe she could bear everyone else's recriminations.

But those were the very people who must hate her the most, she thought. If she tried speaking to them, they would probably spit on her. *And I wouldn't blame them,* she told herself dully. *I wouldn't blame them at all.*

Three

Jessica stepped into Elizabeth's room at a quarter to eight. "PBA meeting at lunch today. You've got to be there."

Elizabeth froze with her arms halfway into the sleeves of a light blue cardigan and stared over her shoulder at her twin. "Jessica, I really don't think anybody will want—"

"You've got to go," Jessica repeated firmly. "It's really important."

PBA, the Pi Beta Alpha sorority, was a sophisticated name for the girls' club of which Jessica was president. They held fund-raising events and attended pep rallies together, but mostly it was an exclusive gossip-exchange. Elizabeth had joined for her twin's sake, but she hardly ever bothered to attend meetings.

With another sharp glance at her sister in the mirror, Elizabeth pulled her sweater on all the way. "Are you serious?" she asked sternly as she fastened the bottom three buttons. "Because I'm in *no* mood to sit around talking about who's dating whom these days, or trying to guess when Lisette's next sale will be."

Jessica's eyes widened with indignation. "Liz, I mean it. Why don't you ever believe me when I say something is important?" With a sullen pout, she turned away.

"I'm sorry, Jess," Elizabeth said, suddenly feeling a little ashamed of herself. "But what's it about?"

"Remember I told you I wanted to do something in Regina's memory? Well, I thought of something."

Elizabeth took two strides to face Jessica and put her hands on her sister's shoulders to look into her eyes. "Oh, Jess, that's great. Tell me what it is."

Jessica shook her head. "Not yet. My plan still isn't totally complete, but it will be by lunchtime. And I need all the Pi Betas to help me. So, will you be there?"

A wave of pride swept over Elizabeth. She had to admit she was really surprised that Jessica was sticking with her plans to make some memorial gesture for Regina. "Of course I'll be there, Jess," she said gently.

"Great. We'll meet in the language lab."

Elizabeth leaned forward and gave her sister a quick hug. "All right, now we'd better get to school, or we'll both miss that meeting."

All the way to school, Elizabeth speculated on what her sister's plan could be. She darted a few surreptitious looks at Jessica as they drove, but Jessica was obviously lost in thought and didn't notice Elizabeth's questioning glances.

Just before homeroom, Elizabeth met up with her best friend, Enid Rollins, by the lockers.

"What's with the look of concentration?" Enid asked lightly, pulling a textbook out of her locker.

With a little shrug, Elizabeth met her friend's green eyes. "Sorry, I guess I was kind of far away."

"Want to talk about it?"

Elizabeth gave Enid a tiny smile. "My sister is planning something. And I know what you're thinking," she added as she caught the doubtful look on Enid's face. There was no love lost between Enid and Jessica. "But she says she wants to do something as a memorial for Regina, and I think she really means it."

At the mention of Regina's name, the sparkle went out of Enid's eyes, and she rubbed her forehead tiredly. "Well, what is it?" she asked finally, her voice low.

"I don't know."

31

"Like a dance? Or—or a plaque or something?"

"I honestly can't imagine. She says she has a plan but won't tell me until the emergency PBA meeting at lunch."

"I don't know how suitable a Pi Beta tribute will be," Enid said. Like Elizabeth, Enid was a member of the sorority in name only, and she shared her friend's opinion about the club mainly being a gossip haven. They started down the crowded hallway, walking slowly as they talked above the noise.

"I know what you mean," Elizabeth said, "but for some reason I get the feeling Jess has thought of something really special this time. I guess we'll just have to wait until the meeting to find out. It's in the language lab during lunch. See you then, OK?" At that moment the first-period bell rang, and the two friends went their separate ways.

Jessica chewed nervously on the edge of her thumbnail as girls began to trickle into the room. She wasn't usually nervous when she was about to give a speech. As much as she loved being president of the sorority, she could admit to herself that the group wasn't always taken seriously, as the science club or the newspaper or the Youth in Government group were. Their reputation for doing "significant" things was not very strong. She just hoped they wouldn't meet a lot of resistance when they tried to put her plan into action.

"Everyone's here," Lila whispered from her left.

"Huh? Oh. Right." Jessica swallowed, then focused on the group of girls in front of her. Their faces were turned toward her with curiosity and sadness. Everyone knew that the meeting had something to do with Regina.

"I—" She cleared her throat and started again, her voice gaining strength as she continued. "I want to thank you all for coming on such short notice, especially when none of us is feeling much like—like doing anything."

She glanced across the room at her sister. Elizabeth's eyes were fixed on her, waiting.

"Anyway," she went on, sitting up a little straighter, "I thought the sorority should do something as a kind of memorial for Regina. I don't want her to be just a memory."

There were a few muffled sniffs, and Jessica noticed her twin pressing her lips tightly together. Enid Rollins reached for Elizabeth's hand and squeezed.

"Some of you might have been aware that when Regina came back from Switzerland, she told Liz all about how wonderful the schools are there and how pretty it is and all, and Liz ended up applying for a scholarship to go to a Swiss boarding school with a special writing program."

An intense silence now filled the room, as every pair of eyes and ears tuned in sharply to her words.

Jessica fidgeted with the gold lavaliere hanging from a chain around her neck and continued. "That scholarship was a memorial scholarship in honor of a very special young girl—a writer—who—who died." She stopped and swallowed hard. Impatiently she wiped away a tear.

"Well, I just thought that when you really look at our school, and all the people who make it special, well, Regina was definitely at the top of the list—"

She was interrupted by a loud sob from Maria Santelli, a cheerleader sitting in the front row. Jean West, another member of the cheering squad, scooted her chair over and put her arm across Maria's shoulders as tears ran down her own cheeks.

"And my suggestion is that we start a college scholarship fund in Regina's memory," Jessica continued, trying to keep her voice steady. "I think it should be an award given to someone who tries as hard as he or she can to overcome some kind of handicap or hardship, just like—like Regina, who never let her deafness get in her way or stop her from doing exactly what she wanted.

"And since the PBAs are so good at raising money, I thought we could organize it and get it started and . . ." Her voice petered out. Jessica sat still, looking at the faces turned toward her. Some of the girls still seemed very sad. But there were looks of growing excitement and eagerness, too.

Across the room Suzanne Hanlon raised her hand. "But, Jessica, doesn't that kind of thing need a lot of administrative work? I mean, do you really think we can handle that?"

"Well, I'm not sure," Jessica admitted. "I think probably what we'd have to do is start a committee of students and faculty and make some kind of list of requirements and draw up an application or something. And then every year that committee would run the scholarship and decide who would get it."

"It could be a special honor committee," Cara suggested. "With only people who are really serious about serving as judges. Maybe the committee could be elected by the student body."

"Yeah, that's right," added Sandra Bacon, her face lighting up with enthusiasm. "And every year people can nominate someone for the scholarship, or maybe people should apply. What do you think, Jess?"

A thrill of excitement rippled through Jessica, and a wide smile spread across her face. She couldn't believe everyone was so responsive to her idea. She met her twin's eyes, and her heart swelled with pride at the look on Elizabeth's face.

"Well, that's something we'll have to straighten out," she said, turning back to Sandra. "There are all kinds of details that have to be settled before this works right. And we probably won't even be able to give the first award until next year, since we're talking about a lot of money."

"How much?" someone asked.

Jessica grimaced. "Well, college is getting pretty expensive these days. I think we should try to make it a few thousand dollars, at least."

There was a stunned silence.

Finally Jennifer Morris, a senior, spoke up. "Where are we going to get that kind of money?"

"Listen," Jessica said, her voice serious, "it's going to mean a lot of work, and we all have to be willing to do it, or else there's no point. And I don't think we should try to do all the fundraising ourselves."

"Everyone in Sweet Valley High will want to help," Elizabeth said quietly. "*Everyone.*"

Jessica nodded at her sister. "It's true. But if you're all willing, I think the sorority should start this and get it as organized as possible. Once it's set up, everyone can help out."

"I'll get my father to donate a *lot* of money," Lila said with sudden intensity. Lila's father was one of the wealthiest men in Sweet Valley. "And I can get money from everyone at the country club, believe me. Everyone there knew Regina."

"And I can get my hands on a lot of movies that we can charge admission for," added Susan Stewart, whose father was a famous film director.

"We can get stores to donate merchandise that we can sell raffle tickets for," someone suggested.

"And put ads in the newspaper."

"We could have a telethon—my mom works at the public TV station."

"Car washes."

"Bake sales."

"We can go door-to-door."

The roomful of girls suddenly dissolved into a number of excited groups as they threw out ideas and talked over the possibilities. In the midst of it all, Jessica fielded questions and jotted down notes on a sheet of paper. It would work. She knew it would.

Elizabeth approached from the back of the room and took her by the hand to lead her aside. For a moment the twins didn't speak. There were tears in Elizabeth's eyes as she looked into Jessica's. "I'm so proud of you, Jess," she whispered. "It's the most wonderful idea you've ever had."

Jessica felt her throat tighten. Few things meant as much to her as Elizabeth's good opinion. "You know," she said, wiping away a tear, "it's a pretty nice feeling, coming up with such a good idea! Maybe I'll do it more often."

"Oh, Jessica!" Laughing and crying at the same time, Elizabeth hugged her. "You know what? I think you're really great."

"Hey. Are you all right?"

Elizabeth looked up and met Jeffrey's clear green eyes. The last bell had sounded, and they were standing on the front steps of Sweet Valley High, the early-afternoon sun throwing their shadows diagonally down the steps.

She swallowed hard and nodded.

"Let's sit down for a second," he suggested, pulling her gently by the hand.

Lost in thought, Elizabeth let him guide her to the far side of the steps. She sat down, still gazing into space.

"You know what I've been thinking?" she began slowly, her brow furrowed with concentration.

"Tell me."

She turned to face Jeffrey and looked at him silently for a moment, her eyes tracing the wave of his sandy hair and the curve of his tan cheek. He was more than just a boyfriend to her: he was a true friend. If anyone would understand her, he would.

"You're going to think I'm crazy," she said with a heavy sigh. "But I keep seeing her everywhere."

"Huh?"

"Regina." She stopped and ran her finger along a tiny branching crack in the marble step as she tried to put her confused and unhappy thoughts into words. "It's just that everywhere I go, I keep thinking I see her. You know, I turn a corner in the hallway, and up ahead is someone with long black hair, and I think to myself, 'Hey, there's Regina. Go catch up with her and see what she's up to.' "

Jeffrey put his arm around her and pulled her to him. "Oh, Liz."

"And then I say, 'You idiot. It isn't Regina.' But I still keep expecting to see her when I turn around." Elizabeth pressed her face into Jeffrey's chest. "And that's why—that's why I—"

"I know."

"I just can't get used to her being gone."

She took a deep breath and wiped her nose with a crumpled tissue. "I want to show you something," she said, sitting up straight and reaching into her book bag. "That poem Nicholas read at the memorial service reminded me how much Regina loved Edna St. Vincent Millay's poetry. This is about a man, but it says just what I mean about Regina."

Elizabeth opened a dog-eared volume of poems to a marked page and silently handed it to Jeffrey. She looked on as he read.

Time does not bring relief; you all have lied
Who told me time would ease me of my pain!
I miss him in the weeping of the rain;
I want him at the shrinking of the tide;
The old snows melt from every mountain-side,
And last year's leaves are smoke in every lane;
But last year's bitter loving must remain
Heaped on my heart, and my old thoughts
    abide.
There are a hundred places where I fear
To go,—so with his memory they brim.
And entering with relief some quiet place
Where never fell his foot or shone his face
I say, "There is no memory of him here!"
And so stand stricken, so remembering him.

Jeffrey sighed. He put his arm around her again and held her close. "It takes time, Liz. It's going to take a lot of time, that's all. There's nothing you can do about it."

Elizabeth said nothing. She let Jeffrey's reassuring strength support her for a while and leaned against him gratefully.

"I think it'll help if you really get involved with this scholarship plan of Jessica's," he said after a while.

Raising her head, Elizabeth gazed into Jeffrey's eyes. "You could be right," she said, managing a faint smile. "I still can't believe Jessica came up with such a great idea."

"Me, either." Jeffrey chuckled softly, then kissed her and held her close.

"We all have to remember Regina in different ways," he continued, stroking her hair. "But the most important thing is that we do remember her."

Elizabeth nodded, and a tear rolled silently down her cheek. "I will. I always will."

Four

Molly closed her locker carefully and swung her book bag over her shoulder. Then she turned and looked up and down the hall: deserted. Waiting until nearly everyone was gone was one way of avoiding people. It was the only thing she could do for self-protection.

Sighing, she walked down the hall toward the front entrance. But as she pushed open the heavy wooden door, she paused. Out on the steps sat Elizabeth Wakefield and Jeffrey French, talking quietly.

Molly took a step backward, out of sight, and watched them for a moment, hating to spy on them but unable to walk out and pass them. She couldn't bear the thought of the looks they

43

would give her. Hopefully they would leave before too much longer.

For a few moments they continued to talk, and then Jeffrey kissed Elizabeth and stood up. "I'll be over later," Molly heard him say.

Elizabeth nodded but stayed sitting on the marble steps. As Jeffrey walked away, Molly frowned, wondering what she should do. For days now, she had felt a strong, compelling need to talk to Elizabeth, to try to apologize, explain what had happened. She knew Elizabeth and Regina had been very close friends. But it was more than that. Elizabeth was one of the few people at Sweet Valley High who might be able to understand what Molly was going through. It was well known that Elizabeth Wakefield could be counted on as sympathetic, honest, and scrupulously fair.

But Molly hesitated. All she could see was Elizabeth's back, but she knew instinctively that Elizabeth was upset. And Molly had a pretty good guess what she might be upset about.

Then Elizabeth stood up.

She's leaving! thought Molly. *I may never get another chance to talk to her alone.*

"Elizabeth! Can I talk to you a minute?" Molly called out, opening the door before she had time to change her mind.

Elizabeth turned, a slight, questioning smile on her face. But when she saw who it was, the smile faded, and her cheeks grew pale.

Molly's stomach turned over when she saw the effect she had on Elizabeth, but she came forward anyway, desperate to talk.

"Molly, I have to go," Elizabeth said, backing away down the steps.

"Wait! Please, Liz. Please don't run away from me yet."

Elizabeth stopped, her expression showing distress and nervousness. "What is it, Molly?"

Pressing a hand to her mouth, Molly tried to organize her thoughts. Now that she was facing Elizabeth, she couldn't think of the right words to convey how she felt about Regina's death. "I just wanted to tell you—to tell you that I never meant—"

Elizabeth shook her head, her eyes bright with unshed tears, and took another step down. "I'm sorry, Molly. I can't talk to you."

"Liz! Please don't—don't hate me," Molly begged pitifully.

There was a long pause. "I don't hate you, Molly," Elizabeth whispered. "But I loved Regina."

Molly clenched her hands together. "Couldn't I—I mean—"

But Elizabeth wouldn't stay any longer. "I'm

sorry, Molly." She turned and ran down the last few steps and headed for the parking lot.

The hope drained from Molly's heart like water from a broken glass. She was left totally empty. In the window of the door, she caught a glimpse of herself: a lost, forlorn figure.

She turned and walked down the steps, her feet moving mechanically, taking her away, away from it all. Without seeing where she was going, without caring whether she would be home late or not, Molly walked the shady, tree-lined streets, and the sound of her footsteps echoed in her ears.

Now that Elizabeth and Justin had turned away, nothing seemed to matter anymore. No one was willing to listen to her, to give her a chance, let her explain what really had happened. There was no one at all to help her cope with the terrible guilt and sadness that was gnawing at her heart.

Cars passed her frequently. She walked unseeing past the middle school and then past the elementary school playground, deaf to the excited shrieks of the children on the swings. A dog trotted by and sniffed at her hand, but Molly never really noticed. Time lost all meaning for her. Her one unconscious thought was that if she just kept walking, maybe somewhere she would find *someone* who would listen to her. She didn't care if she ever got home; she walked all the way to the outskirts of Sweet Valley.

Gradually she became aware of the black iron fence she had been walking along, and there in front of her was a pair of ornate, wrought-iron gates. She swallowed with difficulty, her throat constricted. Without realizing it, she had found her way to the cemetery where Regina was buried.

If anyone would understand, Regina would. And wasn't Regina the one whose forgiveness mattered the most, anyway? She had hardly known Regina at all and had felt a strong resentment toward her because of Justin. But at her party there had been a fleeting moment of connection between them. Regina had come across her suddenly, and their eyes had met: suddenly, it was as if they understood each other completely. It was a moment that had made Molly feel that under different circumstances they might have been friends.

A feeling of relief coursed through Molly. She would talk to Regina and get it all off her chest finally. Maybe then she would be able to face the sentence that the rest of Sweet Valley High had passed on her.

Drawing a deep breath, she pushed open the

gates and stepped into the cemetery. The peace and restfulness of the place immediately surrounded her, soothing her troubled spirit, and she found herself smiling faintly for the first time in days. Towering pine trees threw welcome patches of shade across the sunny lawn, and the grass was soft and springy under her feet. Doves cooed musically from somewhere nearby. She wandered among the graves, searching.

A winding path led her around a clump of evergreen shrubs into a sunlit hollow. And she froze.

Twenty feet away, a young man was kneeling by a fresh grave, facing her but not seeing her. His dark hair tumbled across his forehead, and his handsome face was streaked with tears. It was Nicholas Morrow.

He held a small bunch of roses in his hands. Around him were lavish wreaths and pots full of flowers, already beginning to fade and wilt.

"Regina," he said softly, wiping away a tear. "Why did you do it? Why did you have to go and leave me here all alone? Why did you do it?"

Molly felt like the lowest, most vile spy in the world. Witnessing such grief was terribly wrong, and she knew it. She wished desperately that she could disappear, be anywhere at all besides there, eavesdropping on Nicholas's pain. But she didn't dare make any movement that might catch his eye. All she could do was watch helplessly as he mourned over his sister's grave, and pray that he didn't notice her there.

"Oh, Regina. Why did it have to be you? I told you not to go to that party! I told you!"

He was quiet for a few moments. Then he tenderly placed his bouquet on the ground and dropped his head in despair.

At that, Molly felt a sob rise in her throat, and she took an involuntary step backward to get away from the heart-wrenching scene. There was a loud crack as she stepped on a branch, and Nicholas leaped to his feet.

"Who is it?" he demanded hoarsely. "Who's there?"

Molly was paralyzed with fear. She couldn't let Nicholas find her. But he was walking toward her, his brilliant eyes clouded by misery and anger.

He swept aside the branches that hid her from view, and his face turned deathly white.

For a long, terrible moment, Nicholas and Molly stared at each other, unable to speak. Nicholas's jaw clenched spasmodically, and his eyes were wide with horror.

"How dare you come here?" he whispered, his whole body beginning to shake.

Molly opened her mouth, but no words came out.

"Haven't you done enough damage already? Do you have to make it worse by coming here and—and—" Nicholas was yelling now, outraged by her presence.

"Nicholas—I—"

"Get out of here!" he screamed, raising one hand as if to hit her. "Get out of here and leave us alone! You killed my sister! You killed her!"

A tortured cry escaped from Molly's throat as she turned frantically to run away. She tripped over a root in the path, and fell and scraped her palms. But she didn't feel the pain. She couldn't feel anything but the aching torment of Nicholas's words echoing in her ears.

Somehow, she made it home. There was nothing left for her now. There was no one left to turn to. She was totally alone, in a dark, silent cavern of despair. She shut the door behind her and dragged herself into the living room where she collapsed. The house was utterly quiet: her mother was at her part-time job, her brother was out with his friends, and her father had finally gone back to San Francisco. For a long time she sat there, dazed, until the harsh, insistent ringing of the telephone reached her ears.

Stiffly she began to rise, but then she slumped

back in her chair again. What was the point of answering the phone? she thought.

But it might be her mother, calling from work to make sure Molly had come home from school. She forced herself to answer it.

"Hello?"

There was a brief pause. "Molly. Is that you?"

A warning bell went off in Molly's head. "Who is this?" she asked warily.

"Molly, it's me—your old pal, Buzz."

"What do you want?" she whispered. She gripped the phone to stop her hand from trembling. The last time she had seen Buzz, he had been sneaking out of the house as the police and Nicholas burst in.

"Hey, relax. I just wanted to talk to you—see how you're doing."

"I'm doing lousy, OK? Now leave me alone."

"Molly! Molly, take it easy!" Buzz's voice was smooth, sympathetic. "Hey, I know what you must be going through, and I wanted to see how you are. I was afraid people might be dumping on you pretty bad."

Molly laughed a short, ironic laugh. "Pretty bad?" She threw herself back into the chair, and cradled the phone against her ear. It felt good to hear a sympathetic voice, even if it was just Buzz. She hadn't known him very long, just knew him as a dealer who could always be counted on to turn up at parties with a pocketful of drugs.

"Listen," he crooned. "I know what it's like. A lot of people blame me, too, but hey, who took the drugs, right? It's not like you forced her or anything. It was her own choice. Her own free will."

Molly let Buzz's words wrap around her like a warm blanket. He was on her side. There was actually someone on her side. The relief of it was overwhelming. "You're right," she said hesitantly. "It was her choice."

"Sure! Absolutely. And you know what? I think people should be sticking up for you. After all, the girl goes and dies in your house, right? Gets you in a lot of trouble. That's a real drag. But I bet people don't see it that way, do they?"

"No. They don't." Molly ignored the voice inside her that told her his words rang false. She wanted—*needed*—comfort, and Buzz was giving it freely.

"Well, listen, Molly. I feel really bad for you. I mean it. And you know what? I think there's a lot more to you than people realize. I think you're worth five times what that snotty girl was."

"Oh, I don't—

"Hey," he interrupted her quickly. "I can't

talk anymore now, but I want to see you. I want to see you in person and make sure you're OK."

Molly swallowed hard, tears of gratitude welling up in her eyes. "All right. When?"

"How about tonight, at Kelly's?"

"But aren't the police still looking for you?" Molly asked, feeling a pinprick of doubt. Kelly's was one of the seediest taverns in town, and a frequent spot for police raids.

"Don't worry about that. I'll be in the parking lot out back around ten. Be there, OK?"

"Well—I'll have to sneak out of the house, you know. I'm grounded."

"Figures," he said with a short laugh. "That just makes me even more worried about you, though. No one to talk to, not seeing anybody. I think you'd better come to Kelly's tonight."

It felt so good to have someone concerned about her, to tell her what to do, to make her feel better. She nodded. "I'll be there."

Buzz hung up the phone, he ran a hand through his long, unkempt hair and pulled aside the fly-specked window shade. Through the window he had a great view of the back of another run-down apartment building. Sagging clotheslines were draped between the brick buildings above the alley.

"Man, I can't wait to get out of this dump," he growled, lighting a cigarette. He exhaled smoke on a long sigh. But in order to get out of Sweet Valley, he needed some money. Most of his friends were trying to avoid him. It was only a long overdue favor that had got him the use of this empty apartment for a few days.

And Molly could come in real handy, he thought as he tapped ash onto the windowsill. All he had to do was play it right, and he was out of there.

He glanced at his watch. Four o'clock.

"Six hours to go." He chuckled. "I'll be waiting for you, Molly."

Then he sat back in his chair and closed his eyes, a faint smile on his face.

Five

Jessica gave a muffled sigh of despair. "I can't stand it anymore." She groaned and threw her pencil down on the table in frustration. "I give up."

Spread around her on the kitchen table were her calculator and pages of notes and numbers, most of them illegible with eraser marks and angry scribblings.

Elizabeth lowered the newspaper she was reading and regarded the pages of crossed-out calculations. "Jess, what is this foray into higher mathematics you're making?"

"Please!" Jessica exclaimed, raising her hands in defeat. She scowled at her work and shook her head. "I'm trying to work out how to organize this scholarship fund, and I'm totally lost. I don't know how much we should *try* to raise, how much we *can* raise." She gestured toward one sheet of figures. "Practically every president of every club at school came up to me this afternoon saying they heard about it and that they were going to help raise money. And once we have all that money, I have no idea what we'll do with it. I don't know anything about making investments, finding high-interest accounts."

Her sister just grinned and ducked her head back behind the paper.

"Go ahead and laugh," Jessica went on grumpily, resting her chin in her palm. "But you're not being a lot of help, you know."

"But, Jess, why even bother with that stuff? You should be thinking of ways to *make* the money first, then worry about how to invest it."

Jessica shook her head. "Somebody has to worry about this, you know. As president of the sorority, I feel it's my duty to look into the business aspects of this scholarship."

From behind the paper came a muffled snort.

Jessica scowled again, and she looked around the kitchen, as if searching for inspiration. Her gaze came to rest on the wall clock. "Liz, it's six o'clock! Where's Mom? And why haven't you started dinner yet?" Alice Wakefield's job as a successful interior designer frequently kept her at work late, and the twins often took turns starting dinner.

"Oh, right," came Elizabeth's voice from behind the paper. "Mom called a while ago to say she'd be late and not to start dinner."

Jessica gaped at her twin. "Oh. Thanks for letting me know. What did she mean, though, don't start dinner?"

Elizabeth shrugged.

"Well, I'm starving. What are we supposed to do? Wait indefinitely? We'll just waste away. Are we going out to eat? Is someone coming over for dinner?"

In his basket by the door, Prince Albert looked from Jessica to Elizabeth with concern in his big brown eyes. Then he rose to his feet and crossed the room to Jessica. She felt as if someone had some sympathy for her, even if it was only the dog.

Elizabeth lowered the newspaper and looked Jessica in the eye. "I don't know, Jess. She didn't say. And you can't be starving because you ate a bowl of cereal half an hour ago."

Jessica folded her arms across her chest and pouted. It seemed as if there was only a change in the schedule whenever it was Liz's turn to cook dinner. She never got a break. Not that she minded cooking or doing her share, but there were a lot of things she would rather do. Like reading the latest issue of *Vogue*, playing a game of tennis with Lila up at Fowler Crest, checking out the boys at the Dairi Burger, working on her tan . . .

"Hi, girls. Where's your mom?" Ned Wakefield closed the back door behind him and set his briefcase down on the counter.

Jessica jumped up from the table, ran to him, and grabbed his hand. "She's not home yet, Dad. I need to talk to you about something," she rushed on, dragging him to the table. "Sit down."

"Whoa! Wait a minute. What's all this about?" Her father chuckled as he sat back and loosened his tie. "And what's this mess of paper? It looks the way my office does right before a big trial."

Scooting a chair closer to him, Jessica began. "That's what I need to talk to you about, Daddy. You see, the PBAs are going to start this scholarship fund, and I'm trying to work out how to manage all that money and—"

Mr. Wakefield looked at her curiously as she broke off in midsentence. "Yes?"

"I just heard Mom's car," Jessica cried, bouncing out of her seat. "Now we'll find out what's going on with dinner." She yanked open the door and craned her neck out. "Hi, Mom!"

As Alice Wakefield stepped out of her car, she flashed Jessica a brilliant smile. "Hi, sweetie. Help me with this stuff, will you?"

"What are we having for dinner, Mom?" Jessica called out as she ran down the driveway.

"If you help me with this, you'll find out soon enough."

A pungent, savory odor wafted out of the backseat as soon as Jessica opened the car door. "Mom!" she shrieked excitedly. "You ordered Chinese food!"

Her mother chuckled and shouldered her elegant, soft-leather briefcase. Ducking into the car, she pulled out a paper bag and handed another to Jessica. "Come on," she said with an indulgent smile. "I think we all deserve a treat tonight, don't you?"

"Mom, I need to talk to you about something," Jessica began as she followed her mother to the door. "Ooh, do I smell sweet-and-sour pork?" she interrupted herself and hungrily dug around in the bag, pushing aside the little white cardboard cartons and squishy plastic tubes of duck sauce.

Once inside, Jessica and her mother gratefully dumped their loads on the kitchen table, and Elizabeth and Mr. Wakefield crowded around.

"Mom got Chinese," Jessica explained unnecessarily, as they began opening the cartons.

"I thought this whole family could do with a break," Mrs. Wakefield went on, smiling fondly at her daughters. "We've all been a little down lately. So what do you say we take this feast out to the patio and just have a good time?"

Within minutes, the four had gathered plates, glasses, chopsticks, and napkins and taken them out to the big patio table. Prince Albert followed behind and settled comfortably at Jessica's feet. Everyone concentrated on serving up steaming rice, sweet-and-sour pork, garlic chicken with cashews, sticky spareribs, and spicy sesame noodles. A gentle twilight fell over the backyard, and a soft breeze lapped little wavelets against the side of the swimming pool as they ate.

Afterward, Jessica sat back in her chair and let out a happy sigh. She reached down to stroke Prince Albert's head. "I'm stuffed. That was a great idea, Mom."

Mr. Wakefield popped a chunk of water chestnut into his mouth with his chopsticks. "Mmm. It sure was. Now how about telling us what all that was about before, Jess. Those figures and things."

Once again Jessica was filled with enthusiasm for her plan. She leaned forward eagerly, casting her twin a hopeful smile. Elizabeth grinned back. "Well, you see," she began. "Remember how I wanted to do something for Regina—something to remember her by?"

Her father nodded. "Go on."

"Well, the PBAs are starting a memorial scholarship fund for her. And I need some advice on how to organize it." She went on to explain what they had discussed earlier at the meeting and the trouble she had been having figuring out exactly how to start a scholarship fund.

When she was done, her parents exchanged glances. Then Mrs. Wakefield put her hand on Jessica's arm. "That's a wonderful plan, Jess. I'm very proud of you for coming up with it. And I think the best thing about it is that you're giving the money to someone who has tried hard to overcome some kind of problem or handicap. Those are the people who really deserve help."

A glow of satisfaction spread over Jessica, and she smiled at her mother. Then she turned back to her father.

Mr. Wakefield rubbed his chin and looked thoughtful. Then he nodded emphatically and slapped the table with his open palm. "Jessica, I'm going to offer to administer this fund for you."

"You—you are?" Jessica gasped, taken totally

by surprise. She had counted on help and advice, but not this!

He nodded again. "It's a fairly standard procedure. We handle trust funds of all kinds at the office. I can deal with the banks, research sound investment vehicles, arrange for quarterly reports—"

"Dad!" Elizabeth cut in. "Are you saying you'll run the whole money end?"

"Sure. That is," he added hastily, "if you want me to."

Jessica swallowed with difficulty. If her father managed the finances, she didn't have anything to worry about except handing over the money that the sorority raised. As much as she hated to admit it, she had been feeling a little daunted by the prospect of organizing and running such a project. She had even begun to wonder if she had undertaken more than she could handle. But as usual, something turned up! It always did for Jessica. Across the table, she met her twin's wondering eyes. Elizabeth was as stunned and excited as she was.

"I want you to," she said, letting out a huge sigh of relief. "Just tell me what to do, and I'll do it."

Her father chuckled. "I'll draft a plan for you and your sorority to discuss. If you like what I suggest, we can go ahead with it."

Alice Wakefield beamed at her family and opened the carton of fortune cookies. "Would anyone like to tempt fate?" she asked as she held out the box.

Eagerly Jessica reached in and pulled out the first fortune cookie her fingers touched. She broke it open. And then she instantly burst out laughing.

"Listen to this!" she exclaimed. " 'Today is a good day to make plans'!"

Elizabeth snuggled down on the couch closer to Jeffrey. "You missed a great dinner," she said as she wrapped her arm around his. "Too bad you didn't get here earlier."

"Well, you could have at least saved me a sparerib," he teased her in a fake-whiny tone as he nudged her in the ribs.

She grinned up at him. "Sorry, but it was impossible for this family not to finish a Chinese banquet." She gave him an apologetic kiss on the cheek.

"Hmph."

Settling back on the couch, Elizabeth and Jeffrey turned their attention to the program they were watching on public television. But Elizabeth found she couldn't concentrate very well.

Images of Molly Hecht's distraught face kept swimming into her mind.

"Hey, what's wrong," Jeffrey prodded, sensing her troubled feelings.

"Oh, Jeffrey, I don't know. Something *is* bothering me." She told him about the scene on the front steps and about the look of dying hope in Molly's eyes. "I'm so confused about it. I mean, she was obviously reaching out—for something, and I just couldn't give it. But now . . ." She shook her head, a worried frown creasing her forehead. "Now I don't know what to think. I should have listened to her."

Jeffrey took her hand and held it firmly. "I think I know what you mean. Everyone in school has been shunning her, that's for sure. And I can understand that. But to be perfectly fair, we really shouldn't blame her."

"I know!" Elizabeth agreed quickly. "It's just that . . . well, maybe we're all looking for someone to take our anger and frustration out on. And she's an easy target," she finished, her voice dropping low.

She stared blindly at the TV, recalling Molly's words. *"Don't hate me. Please."* She felt terrible about it but couldn't bear the thought of apologizing to Molly. It was still painful: it still felt wrong to her, no matter how much she tried to understand and be forgiving.

But Elizabeth did hope for Molly's sake that there was someone with a sympathetic ear, someone the girl could turn to for support. If she had a boyfriend, or—

"Justin," Elizabeth said aloud.

"What?"

She turned to look into Jeffrey's eyes. "Before you moved here, Justin Belson and Molly were really close—*really* close, like best friends. I used to see them everywhere together."

"Justin? But he's never with Molly and her crowd anymore. Don't you remember noticing that when Regina started to be friends with him?"

"I know," Elizabeth said, biting her lip. "I guess they drifted apart or something, even though he went to Molly's party. But still, you'd think that for old times' sake. . . ." Her voice trailed off, and she looked down at her hands, which were tightly clenched in her lap. She felt she *had* to do something.

"I'm going to call him," she decided suddenly. "I want to see if there's anything he can do for her."

With a small, lopsided smile, Jeffrey nodded. "Yeah. I guess maybe that's a good idea. Besides," he added, "you won't be able to stop thinking about it until you do."

"You're right," Elizabeth agreed, leaning over

to kiss him on the tip of the nose. Elizabeth jumped up from the couch and pulled the local telephone book from under a stack of newspapers and magazines. She quickly found "Belson, Claire," then dialed the number.

"I know Regina really liked him and thought he was a good guy," she whispered, her hand over the receiver as the ringing sounded in her ear. "Let's hope she was right. She said in her letter she understood how Molly felt, so that must mean that Molly still— Oh, hello, Justin?"

"Yeah."

"This is Elizabeth Wakefield. I was a friend of Regina's."

There was a shocked pause. Then Justin's voice came over the line with a wary edge to it. "Yeah?"

Elizabeth cast an imploring look at Jeffrey. Now that she had the boy on the phone, she didn't really know what to say. She pictured Justin's thin, angular face, his auburn hair sweeping down across his forehead. It was a sensitive, thoughtful face, she thought. He had to be able to help Molly.

"Justin," she began, "I probably don't have any right to butt in like this, but I was talking to Molly today, Molly Hecht—"

"And?" Justin's voice was harsh, even more suspicious than before.

"And I think she really needs a friend right now. She's feeling pretty isolated."

There was silence on the other end.

"Justin?"

"What are you asking me for? She's no friend of mine."

Elizabeth pulled nervously at her gold lavaliere. "Well, you used to be close, didn't you, Justin? I mean maybe she's been acting—I don't know, pretty wild lately—"

"Pretty wild? Elizabeth, I don't think you have any idea what you're talking about."

Stung, Elizabeth stared at the mouthpiece of the phone. Why was he reacting this way? And why was she even bothering? she wondered angrily. But the haunted look in Molly's eyes swam in front of her vision again. She had to try once more to make up for running away from the girl.

"Justin, won't you—"

"No!" he exclaimed, and then, continued in a more subdued tone. "Listen, I really don't want to have anything to do with her anymore. My life got pretty screwed up when we were friends, and I'm trying to get away from all that for good. Don't ask me to go backward."

Elizabeth shook her head. There wasn't really anything more she could do, it seemed. "Well, OK. I'm sorry for bothering you."

"No problem."

The phone went dead in her hand, and Elizabeth replaced the receiver carefully. Looking up, she met Jeffrey's questioning gaze, and she shrugged. "He said no. But anyway, maybe I was imagining things when I thought she needed help," she said.

He looked at her for a moment and nodded. "Yeah, maybe you were."

But as Elizabeth tried to focus on the television drama again, she had an uncomfortable suspicion that she had been right about Molly after all. The girl needed help—and soon.

Six

Molly stared hard at her reflection in the bathroom mirror. Staring back was a thin, pinched face filled with confusion, bewilderment, and pain. But even as she watched, her mouth settled into a grim line of acceptance. *This is the way it's going to be from now on*, she told herself bitterly.

She glanced at her watch: nine-forty. She would have to leave soon if she was going to meet Buzz as they had planned. All her instincts were crying out, telling her not to go, not to turn to Buzz. But the memory of his comforting voice lulled her into ignoring the warnings.

Quietly she slipped back into her bedroom

and closed the door behind her, listening. From down the hall she could hear the muffled sound of her mother's favorite radio station. Her mother usually was asleep by this time on the days she worked, exhausted from getting up at six for her two-hour commute. If all went well, she would never even know Molly wasn't in her own bed.

After shrugging into her denim jacket, Molly raised the window and paused. Still no sound. Taking a deep breath, she hitched herself up onto the sill and swung her legs around. Then she pushed off and dropped noiselessly to the ground, grateful that she lived in a one-story ranch house. She dusted off her knees and stood quickly, then trotted away from the house without a backward glance.

Cars swept past her on the road as she hurried along. Their headlights glared in her eyes every time she turned to stick out her thumb. Finally one stopped, and she climbed in gratefully.

"Where are you going?" asked the driver, a tired-looking middle-aged man.

"On the state road. Kelly's."

He glanced at her but didn't say anything. Before too long, they saw a flashing neon sign up ahead marking the sleazy roadside tavern. Molly sighed with relief. As the car stopped by a streetlight, she checked her watch: it was ten o'clock.

"Thanks a lot," she said as she hopped out.

The car pulled away, and Molly glanced nervously around her. "Buzz, you'd better be here," she muttered. She had been to Kelly's plenty of times before, but never to meet a fugitive from the police. The parking lot was full, and she could hear the steady beat of a bass from inside the bar.

Cautiously Molly wandered among the cars, wondering how she was going to find Buzz. Then a voice hissed out through the darkness. "Molly! Over here!"

There was a strident creak as the door of a beat-up green Camaro swung open. Buzz's face was visible as he leaned out into the faint glow from the streetlights. He was grinning as Molly hurried over.

"Hey, Mol. You came."

"Of course I came," she retorted breathlessly as she climbed in beside him on the cracked vinyl seat. "I said I would and I did, OK?"

He chuckled softly. "OK, don't get hyper. I'm just really glad, that's all."

Molly nodded and shivered slightly from the built-up tension.

"Hey, you're not scared, are you?" Buzz took her hand firmly and caressed it.

"No." She sighed. Drawing a deep breath, she added, "It's been a pretty hairy week, though."

71

"I know what you mean. Listen" —Buzz looked over his shoulder through the rear window at the tavern's side door—"why don't you go on in and get us some brews so we can relax. It's been a tough week for both of us." He glanced back at her sharply. "Got any money?"

"I think so," Molly said. She leaned forward into a patch of light and dug in her purse with both hands. "Yeah, I've got a few dollars." Opening the car door she added, "I'll be right back."

The gravel of the parking lot crunched under her feet as she walked past the cars. Bits of broken glass twinkled in the dim light, and from inside the bar came a raucous burst of laughter and shouting. She pushed open the door and stepped inside.

The air was thick with cigarette smoke, and a deafening country-western song pulsated from the flashing jukebox. Molly smelled stale beer, sweat, and grease as she pushed her way through the crowd around the bar. She ignored the appraising looks sent in her direction. "Can I have a couple bottles of Miller?" she shouted above the din.

The bartender, a puffy-eyed man with a stained apron stretched over his paunch, quirked one eyebrow at her skeptically. Molly tried to make herself look taller and met his eyes defiantly, willing him to serve her. But underage drinkers were commonplace there, and without a word, he opened two bottles set them on the counter, then gave her change for the bills she put down.

As she shoved her way back to the door, a vaguely familiar voice caught her ear, and she slowed down to listen.

"Yeah, he's still hiding out," the guy she recognized as a friend of Buzz's was saying. "He showed up at some Mickey Mouse high-school party, and some stupid kid got herself killed doing coke. *I* sure don't know where he is, but I know a few cops who'd really like to find out."

There was a chorus of laughter, and Molly shuddered involuntarily. It seemed to be a joke to them, just an annoying inconvenience their pal was going to have to get around. She pushed her shoulder against the door and stepped outside again into the night air.

For a moment she stood on the step and rubbed her forehead with one cold bottle of beer. Her head was pounding—from the noise, the stuffy air, the anxiety of the past two weeks. She felt awful and wished desperately for some peace.

"Molly! Come on!" Buzz's voice lashed out across the parking lot. She ran over to the

Camaro and clambered in with the beers clutched in one hand.

"Great, I really need this brew," Buzz said with a low chuckle. He pulled thirstily at the bottle and then lowered it. He regarded Molly. "You're not drinking," he noticed. "Go on. Bottoms up."

Molly curled her mouth in a self-mocking smile. "Yeah. I guess I should." With a deep breath, she tilted up the bottle and drank deeply, feeling the cold beer race down her throat and into her stomach. Almost at once she felt a soothing tingle, and she was glad she hadn't eaten any dinner. *All the faster to get drunk*, she thought.

She heaved a weary sigh. Closing her eyes, she leaned back against the headrest. Next to her, she felt Buzz slide closer and put a hand on her leg.

"You know, Molly, the more I get to know you, the more I think you're a really special person. You know that?" His voice crooned in her ear, and his breath was warm against her neck.

"Really?" she mumbled. It was heaven to be hearing a warm, sympathetic voice for a change, and Molly was grateful that the beer was already doing its work.

"That's right. I think we're a lot alike. People don't understand you, right? They come down on you all the time, criticize you. Am I right?"

She stiffened involuntarily as she thought of how she had been treated lately. Just the thought of it brought the pain rushing back. She tipped up her beer bottle and drank again.

"Yeah," she whispered finally. "That's true. How did you know?"

He stroked her arm. "Because I feel like I've known you all my life. Honest. I've never felt this way about anyone, Molly. I—I really mean it."

Molly turned and looked into his eyes. They were dark and fathomless in the dim light that bathed the inside of the car. His thin face was shadowed, too, and she felt a momentary panic as she had a vision of his sneering mouth and eyes the night Regina died. *What are you doing here with him?* her mind screamed. Then, as he bent forward and kissed her, she pushed the thought out of her mind and let herself melt against him. It didn't matter who he was. He was treating her with a warmth it seemed she hadn't felt in ages.

"Oh, Molly," he whispered against her hair. "Molly, Molly, baby. Nobody understands you like I do."

Her head sank down to rest on his shoulder, and Molly felt tears spring to her eyes. But for once, they were tears of happiness, instead of tears of pain and loneliness. "Oh, Buzz. I've really been having a rough time lately."

"I know," he crooned. "I know. And I've got just the thing to make you feel better."

"Huh?" Molly sat up straight, trying to focus on his face. Her head was beginning to feel fuzzy.

"That's right. Everybody's best friend. Here." Buzz was holding a joint in his hand, and Molly saw herself reach for it. "That's right," he continued, lighting a match and watching the end flare up and take hold.

Molly breathed deeply, pulling the marijuana smoke down into her lungs. A faint voice inside her told her she was being crazy, that this was what had started it all in the first place. But she ignored it. She took another long drag, then passed the joint to Buzz as a peaceful feeling of relaxation flooded through her. She didn't care if it was wrong or stupid or that the boy next to her was wanted by the police. She just wanted to forget everything, ignore the world, let it fade away.

"Mmm . . . escape." She sighed and leaned back against the seat.

Buzz turned quickly to look at her, his eyes huge and black in the darkness. "What did you say?"

"Escape." She giggled.

A slow smile spread over his face, but he grew serious again in a moment, and he took her hand in his. "Molly, you know, I never thought I'd say this to a girl, but I really need you. I feel something deep and real for you. We belong together, but—"

"But what?" Molly said after a long pause, her voice thick and slurred.

He shook his head. "But I've got to split, Mol. The cops are after me, you know? I've got to get out of this town and stay out."

Molly tried to swallow, but her mouth was too dry. She brought her beer bottle to her lips and sipped the last few drops. There was something he was trying to tell her, but she couldn't make her brain concentrate. "I—I don't understand," she said thickly.

"Oh, Molly! Just when we've found each other. That's the way life treats people like us. After all these years I've finally found somebody like you, and I've got to leave you. Damn! It's so unfair!"

"But—"

He pounded the steering wheel angrily and scowled through the windshield. "If only—no, forget it. It's impossible." He ran a hand through his hair in a gesture of angry frustration.

"If only what?"

Turning, he took her face in his hands and

looked deeply into her eyes. Molly felt as if he were staring straight into her soul. "If only you could come with me, then we'd always be together. But I can't ask you to do that. Just forget I ever said anything." He dropped his hands and stared ahead again but darted one or two quick looks at her from the corner of his eye.

As if from far away, Molly heard her voice saying, "I could come with you."

Buzz gaped at her, astonished. "No! I couldn't ask you to run away—no."

Molly shook her head, trying to dispel the fog of pain and confusion. What was she saying? Was she totally crazy?

But instead of rejection, here was an offer of something more, something better. And it was coming from someone who said he wanted her. She hadn't heard much of that lately. "There's nothing to keep me here," she said, rubbing her tired eyes with the heel of her hand.

"Would you do that for me? Honest? Now that you mention it, it might be a really good idea. Of course, you'll come back home."

"How come?"

He snorted. "Listen, when the people here know you're gone, they're going to realize what a big mistake they made treating you so bad. They'll be so sorry they ever dumped on you this way. They'll be begging you to come home, believe me."

Faces and voices swam into Molly's imagination—angry faces, harsh voices accusing her of tormenting Regina Morrow and driving her to her death. How dare they treat her that way? Well, she would show them. She would show them what they'd get for treating her so badly.

A sob welled up in her throat. "Those—those pigs," she choked. "I can't think of anything bad enough to call them! But they'll see. I'll show them. I'm going with you, Buzz. They'll be sorry. All of them."

She pictured her parents, their faces growing hot and red with fury when they discovered her absence. *It served them right*, she thought, hastily wiping away a tear. And that goody-goody Elizabeth Wakefield and Regina's snotty brother.

"You're right. I don't have to stay here and take their abuse," she said, facing Buzz defiantly. "Where are you going?"

Drawing a deep breath, Buzz shook his head. "I don't know. South, I guess. Maybe we could get to San Diego and then cross the border into Mexico. I've got to lay low for a while, let the heat cool off a little. Those cops are really on my tail, but they'll give up if we make it hard enough."

Suddenly Molly saw clearly what she and Buzz were planning, and an ice-cold wave of dread washed over her. As if he sensed her reluctance, Buzz wrapped his arms around her tightly. "You and me, Molly. We belong together. I know how to treat you right, take care of you. Here." He handed her the joint.

When he passed the marijuana to her, Molly suffered a moment of indecision. She could take it all back now, she knew. Or go forward. This was the moment of truth.

She inhaled deeply, wishing she didn't have to choose, wishing the world would just recede into a pinpoint of nothingness. Then she handed it back to him.

"The only thing is," he went on, his voice gentle and soothing, "I need some cash. Do you have any money, Molly?" he asked quietly, staring into her eyes.

She nodded, mesmerized. "I've got a couple thousand dollars in a savings account downtown."

He drew in his breath sharply. "Can you get it? I mean, without anyone knowing?"

"Sure. It's my money, and I've got the passbook. I've been saving for—" She broke off. She had been saving for college since she was little, since before her life got so messed up. College seemed so remote now. In fact, she hadn't even really thought about it in years. It was just a dream she'd had a long time ago. But it didn't seem to matter now. Nothing seemed to matter except getting away from Sweet Valley and everyone who was persecuting her and making her life so miserable.

"It was her own fault," Molly said unconsciously. "It was her own fault."

"That's right," Buzz agreed. He handed her the joint again and guided her limp hand up to her mouth. "So can you get the money? And meet me here tomorrow around eight?"

She stared at him blankly.

"OK, Molly?" His eyes bored into hers, and he leaned forward to kiss her again hungrily. "I need you, Molly," he whispered, his voice urgent. "Say yes. *Say yes.*"

"All right, Buzz. Whatever you say."

Seven

Jessica was just clearing her breakfast dishes when there was a knock at the door. A quick glance at the wall clock told her it was half past seven, and she raised her eyebrows in surprise.

"Who could that be?" she muttered. The only people who came to the back door were people who knew them fairly well. She reached for the handle, curious.

Standing on the doorstep was Nicholas Morrow, looking more handsome than ever in spite of the worried crease lining his aristocratic forehead. Jessica smiled with pleasure and automatically smoothed her short denim skirt over her hips.

"Hi, Nicholas. Come in."

He gave her a half-hearted smile and stepped inside the bright, sunny kitchen. "Hi, Jess. Is Liz still here?"

"Still here?" She gave him an amused look as she closed the door behind him. "Yeah, I think it's a safe bet at this time of the morning."

He started guiltily. "Oh, I'm really sorry. I—I didn't even realize it was so early. I need to see Liz, though."

The air of little-boy forlornness on Nicholas's face stopped Jessica from teasing any further. "Sit down, Nicholas. I think Liz'll be down in a minute. Want some coffee or something?"

"Thanks." Nicholas pulled out a chair and sat.

Jessica poured a mug of coffee for him and sat opposite him, suddenly at a loss for something to say. Usually she had no problem talking to a gorgeous boy, but for some reason, Nicholas's attitude kept her silent. She guessed he was brooding over Regina.

"Say, Nicholas," she began tentatively. "My sorority is starting a memorial scholarship fund for Regina."

Slowly his eyes focused on her face. "I'm sorry, Jess. What did you say?"

Jessica bit her lower lip and pleated a paper napkin nervously. She was beginning to wonder if this was the right time to tell him. He sure was acting strangely.

"Jessica? I'm sorry, I didn't hear what you said."

"Well, I just wanted to tell you that my sorority is planning to start a memorial scholarship fund. In memory of Regina." She looked anxiously into his face and was relieved when he broke into a beautiful, tender smile.

"You're kidding? That's really—that's so sweet of you, Jessica," he said, warming her with his look of gratitude. "Thank you," he said simply. "Thank you so much."

A tingle of pleasure rippled through Jessica as she returned his electrifying smile. From the first, she had been attracted to Nicholas and had tried every trick she could think of to focus his attention on her. But he had zeroed in on Elizabeth, who wasn't at all interested in him romantically. At the time, she had still been deeply involved with her boyfriend, Todd, and no amount of Nicholas's attention could shake that. Now, the two were just very good friends; and Jessica knew that Nicholas often confided in her sister. He was an awfully nice boy, she realized with a twinge of envy.

She flashed Nicholas a brilliant smile as he met her eyes again, and she assumed a thoughtful expression. "You see, we thought—well, to tell you the truth, it was my idea," she admitted modestly. "I thought it would be a great way to remember how brave and determined Regina was." She glanced up quickly through her eyelashes to gauge his reaction. "I hope you don't mind."

"Mind?" An incredulous smile spread over Nicholas's face. "Jessica, how could I mind such a considerate gesture?" He reached across the table for her hand and took it in his own. "It really means a lot to me. And I know my parents will be very touched."

"I'm trying to put it all together right now. There's so much to organize," she hurried on. "But I think I'll be able to manage."

"I'm sure you will," he responded warmly.

Just then Elizabeth pushed open the door from the hall.

"Nicholas!"

Instantly he leaped to his feet, and Jessica knew she had been forgotten. Hiding her disappointment, she stood up. "Well, see you later."

But Elizabeth and Nicholas were staring at each other with a strange, communicative look, and neither noticed her. Jessica shrugged and left the room.

"Liz," Nicholas began haltingly. "Liz, I really need to talk to you. Can I drive you to school?"

The look of intense concentration on his face took Elizabeth by surprise. But she knew him well enough to realize that he had something important on his mind. Over the course of their relationship, what had started as a strong romantic attraction had mellowed into a warm, caring friendship. They had spent many long hours talking about Regina and talking about their own dreams and ambitions.

She made a quick decision. "Sure, Nicholas. Let me get my things." Darting out into the front hall, she grabbed her book bag and a light jacket, then rejoined him in the kitchen. "Let's go."

Nicholas took her arm, steered her toward his Jeep, and politely opened the door for her. She stepped in and, with some difficulty, forced herself to be quiet and not to ask the questions that rose to her lips. She knew instinctively that she would have to wait for him to begin.

After a few minutes of silence, Nicholas ran a hand through his hair and sent her a quick glance. "Something really awful happened yesterday, Liz. It just makes me sick when I think about what I did."

With half his attention on the traffic, Nicholas

recounted the scene in the graveyard with Molly Hecht. His voice was controlled and steady, but Elizabeth sensed he was badly shaken by the incident.

"What really got me," he finished, "is how I reacted. I mean, I laid into her as if she had taken a gun to Regina's head and pulled the trigger. I know it wasn't like that, but I couldn't stop myself!" He pounded the steering wheel in agitation. "I just totally lost control."

Elizabeth swallowed hard, remembering her own reaction to Molly the previous afternoon. "I know what you mean," she said. "I guess we're all looking for someone to take our anger and sadness out on."

"You're right. I mean, I know that Molly isn't really responsible for what Regina did. But when I saw her there, I just went wild. I should have been more mature about it, I guess."

"No one could blame you, you know. I can understand why it would be such a shock to see her there, especially when you were so upset about Regina." She stared out the window, commanding her mind not to call up a picture of Regina's face.

They were silent for a few minutes, and Elizabeth fiddled unconsciously with a ballpoint pen, clicking it open and shut over and over. "What did you? . . ." she began hesitantly.

Nicholas gave her a rueful smile. "You think I want you to take care of it for me, right? Clean up after my stupid blunder?"

Blushing, Elizabeth looked out the window. "No, I—"

But Nicholas interrupted her. "I just thought if you see Molly today in school, you might tell her I'm sorry." At eighteen, Nicholas was working for a year in his father's computer business before going to college, and as a result, he had very little contact with most of the Sweet Valley High crowd. "If I can track her down, I'll apologize myself, but for the time being . . ."

"Sure, no problem," Elizabeth replied automatically. But inside, she was thinking fast, and she didn't like what she knew was the truth. Ever since Regina's death, the entire school had been ostracizing Molly, and she herself was just as guilty as the rest of them. Treatment like that had to have an effect on a person, and Elizabeth began to see what Molly must have been going through.

And on top of all that, Molly had tried to reach out to her yesterday. There had been true sorrow and regret in the girl's eyes. A flood of shame washed over Elizabeth as she remembered her own reaction. Molly hadn't been feeling sorry for herself, she realized. And now after what Nicholas had told her, she felt even worse. After she had turned her back on Molly, Molly had obviously sought refuge in the cemetery. Elizabeth's throat constricted at the thought of Molly seeking out the one person who couldn't reject her, the one person who would have understood. It was desperately pitiful.

But clearly, Molly hadn't found any sympathy there. Instead, she had faced a torrent of abuse from Regina's brother.

"Oh, God, Nicholas. What have we done?" Elizabeth said.

"I think we've all gone too far," he answered, his eyes clouded with remorse. "I wish there was something we could do."

With a powerful roar, the Jeep swept up the curve of the school driveway and came to a stop near the wide marble staircase. For a moment neither of them spoke. Then Elizabeth pulled herself together and cast him a quick, fleeting smile. "I'll see what I can do," she said, her voice gentle. "And listen, don't beat yourself over the head about what you did, OK?"

He turned in his seat and met her eyes. "OK, Liz," he said after a moment. He reached for her hand and held it briefly. "And thanks a lot."

"No problem." With another smile, she opened her door and climbed out. "See you later."

Lost in thought, Elizabeth stood at the bottom of the stairs, absently watching Nicholas drive away. She was more disturbed about the situation than she wanted to admit, and she was confused as to what she should do—if anything. *The girl has her own friends*, one side of Elizabeth coaxed. Then the other side of her conscience reminded her that every one of Molly's friends had deserted her.

Elizabeth walked slowly up the steps and thought about what to do. Nicholas hadn't exactly put her in a great position. Well, she'd been feeling bad enough about her own confrontation with Molly, so the only thing to do was seek her out and apologize, find out how she was doing.

She pushed through the doors into the crowded hall and slung her book bag over her shoulder. As she headed for her locker, she caught a glimpse of Molly down the hall hovering around the water fountain. The girl's face was drawn and haggard, as though she hadn't slept in days. *Now's your chance*, Elizabeth thought, but somehow she couldn't bring herself to approach Molly. Surely she would see her again later, between classes, during lunch. She would talk to her then. With a sigh she took her chemistry book from her locker and rushed off as the bell was ringing.

Elizabeth kept her eyes open for Molly all morning and her ears open for any conversations about the girl. Time didn't seem to be softening anyone's opinion of Molly Hecht's role in Regina's death. In the halls between classes, Elizabeth caught scraps of conversation now and then about Molly and Regina. The tragedy was still the main topic of conversation at Sweet Valley High, and no one was easing up in their harsh judgment of the case. It was enough to convince Elizabeth that it would be a long time before anyone would have sympathy for Molly.

At one point, Elizabeth did spot Molly. She was staring vacantly out a window, and Elizabeth's heart went out to her. She ached to do something, but she just didn't feel she knew Molly well enough to reach out to her. And she also suspected that after the way she had responded to Molly yesterday, her efforts wouldn't make much difference. Regardless of what she had told Nicholas, she wasn't sure Molly would be very receptive to an apology on his behalf, either. To be perfectly fair, Elizabeth didn't think *she* would, in Molly's position. So she still kept her distance.

Furthermore, Elizabeth's conscience was waging war on her. Did she owe her loyalty to her departed friend? Or should she try to help a girl she hardly knew at all, a girl she still, deep down, felt was responsible for Regina's death?

But Elizabeth refused to believe there was nobody to help Molly. There had to be someone, and she had an idea who that might be. Even if he had already said no.

Eight

Justin scowled at the blank notebook open in front of him. Five pages on Hamlet's soliloquy due the day after tomorrow, and he hadn't even started. The blank paper seemed to mock him and made it impossible for him to write anything at all.

But what was the point, anyway? he asked himself distractedly. A couple of weeks ago there had seemed to be a good reason to try to do well in school. Now . . . well, what difference did it make? Who cared?

He stared morosely around the library. Through the window he could see Ken Matthews and Winston Egbert clowning around on the front lawn with a Frisbee. A group of girls stood nearby laughing behind their hands; some boys from the tennis team called out jokes to one another on their way to the courts.

Why isn't my life like that? he wondered. *Why can't I ever be like them?* He grasped his pencil so hard it snapped in two in his hands, making him jump. Shaking his head in disgust, he tossed the two pieces onto the table and slumped down farther in his chair. He would never have a life as free of real problems as those kids' lives were. How could he, with a pill-popping mother and no father at all? *Everything I touch falls apart.*

"Well, forget it. Just forget it. I don't need this junk," he muttered grimly.

He was about to stand up and abandon his books there on the table when he heard a tentative cough from behind him. Turning slowly in his chair, he found Elizabeth Wakefield looking at him nervously.

His eyes narrowed as he guessed what she was there for. "Listen, Elizabeth. I already told you—"

"May I sit down?" she broke in, quickly pulling out a chair across from him. "*Hamlet*, huh? Isn't it a great play?"

He eyed her warily. "I guess so. I don't know."

Keeping her eyes on the book, Elizabeth continued, "Having trouble with an English paper?"

He said nothing, and she went on in a rush as he fiddled with the broken pencil. "Then maybe we can help each other out. Make a deal."

Justin took a deep breath. "What kind of deal?" he asked, rubbing his hands on his pants. He felt a pinprick of nervousness, as though something was going to happen that he had no control over.

"What kind of deal?" he repeated.

She looked up then, her blue-green eyes meeting his steadily. "I'll help you write your paper if you help me out with Molly."

Giving Elizabeth a disgusted grimace, Justin pushed his chair back and tensed himself to stand.

"Please listen to me, Justin. For five minutes, that's all." The urgency in her voice penetrated Justin's wall of anger, and he waited for her to go on.

Elizabeth licked her lips and leaned forward across the table. "I know how you feel about Molly—we all feel that way. But it's wrong. Don't you see? If by turning our backs on Molly we ruin her life, then Regina won't have been the only loser in all this."

Justin's heart began to pound, and he saw again Regina's pale face, heard her shallow, rasping breaths as she lapsed into a coma. Mutely he shook his head.

"It's wrong!" Elizabeth grabbed his hand to keep him from rising. "I may not know Molly at all, or what her life is like, but I know that wrecking it is wrong. Somebody has to tell her that it wasn't her fault—*because it wasn't*. Justin, it wasn't her fault!"

Something about Elizabeth reminded Justin painfully of Regina. Maybe it was the sincerity, the honest, uninhibited desire to do the right thing. She was willing to ignore the stereotyped boundaries that kept most of the kids at Sweet Valley High separated into cliques. Regina had accepted him for who and what he was; she didn't care if their lives were worlds apart.

And now Elizabeth was saying the same thing. No wonder the two girls had been so close.

"I don't understand something," he said hoarsely, giving her a searching look. "Why do you care what happens to Molly Hecht?"

There was a long, tense pause, and Elizabeth sighed wearily. "A week ago I probably would have said I didn't care. But things are different now."

"What's different? Nothing's changed. Regina's still dead!"

She looked at him bleakly. "I know. That's

why we have to help Molly, because hurting her won't bring Regina back. And she really needs help, Justin. You can tell just by looking at her that she's near the breaking point."

"Well, whose fault is that, huh?" Justin's voice was bitter, and he turned his face away from her. "She's the one who got so heavily into drugs. She's the one who started this whole thing in motion."

"Maybe. But maybe it got this far because no one tried to stop her—"

"I did try."

With a look of true compassion, Elizabeth shook her head. "But *why* did you try? Because you cared about her, right? Don't you still care enough to try again?"

Justin felt tired and defeated. He wished he could just curl up and hide, far from everything around him. All the years he and Molly had been friends—and they had been the best of friends—Molly had helped him cope with the pain of losing his father. Now he felt completely alone.

A scene came back to him with startling clarity, so fresh it seemed as if it had happened only yesterday, although it was really a couple of years before. One crisp autumn day, he and Molly had cut school and gone up to Secca Lake together. On the shore they had found a small wood duck with an injured wing. It hardly struggled at all as Molly picked it up and smoothed back the glossy feathers. She wrapped the little duck gently in her sweater and took it to the ranger station, where the ranger said he would make sure it was looked after. Justin knew he would remember that day as long as he lived.

He swallowed with difficulty. "I'll think about it, Liz. I've got to think about it for a while."

"Justin—"

"I *said* I'd think about it." His voice was tight and hard, and Justin felt ashamed of himself for acting so immaturely. But he couldn't help it. He turned away, not wanting to meet her eyes. "I'll think about it, Elizabeth. That's all I can say."

She nodded slowly. "All right. I'm going to see if I can find her now. There's no reason for me to keep making excuses for myself anymore. I realize that. I just don't know if she'll listen to me." Elizabeth pushed herself up from the table and gave him a faint smile. "And I meant what I said about helping you with your paper," she continued. "If you want me to."

"Thanks." Justin looked away again through the window. "I'll talk to you later."

When he knew she was gone, Justin dropped

his head down onto his arms. Would Molly listen to *him*? After the way he had rejected her, he didn't have much faith in his ability to get through to her. He pounded the table with his fist. "Why can't I ever do anything right?" he whispered to himself. "Why?"

"So then he held my hand and told me how much he liked the idea," Jessica said, popping a french fry into her mouth. "Do you think there's any hope for me? With Nicholas, I mean."

"Oh, give me a break, Jess." Lila arched one eyebrow. "You know perfectly well that Nicholas is just one of the most polite guys in town, that's all. He doesn't mean anything by it. People with breeding are always very gallant."

Jessica shrugged. "It was just a thought. Boy," she went on, changing the subject, "this scholarship business is going to be a lot of work, you know."

Lila took one of Jessica's fries and dragged it through the pool of catsup. "Can we just drop the subject for a while? I have to tell you something. Guess who I saw together yesterday?"

Both Jessica and Cara leaned a little closer. "Who?" Cara asked, as casually as she could. She used to be an incurable gossip, but Jessica knew her friend was trying to be better. It was pretty difficult, though, when Lila didn't feel any constraint about it at all.

Lila smiled. "Well, I was on my way—"

"Just get to the point, Lila," Jessica commanded impatiently.

"Oh, all right," Lila said, looking slightly wounded. "I saw Sandy Bacon with that guy Manuel Lopez. And they looked pretty friendly, let me tell you."

"Manuel Lopez? That Mexican guy? He's a senior, isn't he?"

Lila shook her head impatiently. "No, he's a junior, but that's not the point, Cara! Geez, you can be dense."

"The point is," Jessica cut in, resting her chin in her hands, "that Sandy's parents are really prejudiced. Remember how embarrassed she was when her father wrote that letter to the editor of the *Sweet Valley News* about how the town was being 'overrun' by immigrants? He's a real bigot." Jessica pictured the pretty blond cheerleader and smiled as she imagined her with the darkly handsome Manuel.

Cara nodded slowly, biting her lip in concentration. "Well, so what do you think's going on, Lila?"

"It's not for me to say," Lila said primly. But she grinned again and cast a quick look around the cafeteria. "Hey, Jess, here comes Liz."

102

Jessica looked up quickly as her twin maneuvered her way past the tables toward her. An anxious crease lined Elizabeth's forehead, and Jessica knew something was really troubling her.

"Jess, hi. Hi, Cara, Lila." Elizabeth smiled at them distractedly and sat down next to Jessica. "Listen, have you seen Molly Hecht recently?"

"What?" Jessica's voice rose up indignantly. "What are you looking for *her* for?" She was mortified that her sister was actually seeking out Molly, and she cast a surreptitious glance across the table. Cara and Lila both were staring openmouthed at Elizabeth.

"Yeah," Cara put in. "What do you want with her?"

Elizabeth brushed a lock of hair back behind her ear. "I need to talk to her, that's what. I think everybody has been treating her really rottenly over this whole business about Regina, and I wanted to apologize—"

"Apologize?" interrupted Lila. "For what? What do you have to apologize to *her* for?"

Elizabeth ignored her. "Listen, she came to me yesterday, and I was really cold to her. Now I think it was wrong of me."

Jessica shook her head incredulously. "Elizabeth Wakefield, I can't believe you are my own twin sister. And to tell you the truth, I think it's pretty lousy of you to try to be nice to Regina's murderer. It's as if you don't even *care* about Regina anymore." She shut up when her twin glared at her fiercely.

"Jessica, I'm going to pretend I didn't hear you say that."

The tension around the table mounted as Jessica and Elizabeth stared at each other. Finally Cara cleared her throat. "Actually, Liz, I was in the main office just before lunch, and I heard her asking one of the secretaries which bus went past the Union Bank. I mean, I don't know, but maybe she's on her way there now."

Drawing a deep breath, Elizabeth turned away and stood up. "Thanks, Cara."

Jessica grabbed her sister's wrist. "You're not actually going to go look for her, are you?"

"Yes, I am." Gently Elizabeth took Jessica's hand off her arm. "There's a lot more to this than you realize, Jess. And if you thought about it for a while, you might understand. I *have* to find Molly. It may already be too late."

As Jessica and her friends watched speechlessly, Elizabeth walked away and out the cafeteria door. Once she was out of sight, Jessica turned to the others. "Too late for what? I don't know what she's talking about."

"Wow, this is really weird," Lila said, turning wide eyes to them. "Liz going to apologize to Molly Hecht, of all people."

"Maybe she knows something we don't know," Cara suggested with a puzzled frown.

"Yeah," grumbled Jessica, licking the salt off her fingers. "Maybe." Her eyes strayed to the door again as she wondered what her sister was up to.

Nine

The bus door hissed shut as Molly jumped down to the sidewalk. Squinting her eyes against the bright sunlight, she waited for a break in the busy lunch-hour traffic. Then she dodged across the street and into the cool sanctuary of the Union Bank.

Once inside, though, the momentum that had brought her this far gave out, and Molly stopped, unable to take the next step. The ceiling arched away up above into dimness, and pale sunlight filtered in through high, vaulted windows. A cathedral-like hush filled the huge space, making her feel small. Across the room was a line of tellers' booths. If she was going to go through with it, she had to do it now.

Her heels clicked softly on the marbled floor as she crossed to a table for a withdrawal slip. "It's our ticket to Mexico," she told herself firmly. "We can't get out of here without the money. We've got to have that money."

Willing herself to keep her hand steady, she copied out her account number from the passbook. But her hand moved more and more slowly until finally she was motionless. She stared at the slip under her pen.

"Miss, can I help you?"

She jumped guiltily and looked up into the bank guard's inquisitive face. "N-no," she stammered, her cheeks flushing hotly. "I—I just couldn't remember how much money I needed, that's all."

He smiled uncertainly at her and backed away. Molly imagined that she could feel his eyes boring steadily into her back.

He knows what I'm doing! she thought wildly. *He knows about me and Buzz. He's going to arrest me.*

Then she pulled herself together and chided herself sternly for panicking. Calmly she flipped the passbook open to the last page and read the balance: $2,314.83. She picked up the pen again and wrote $2,314.83 in the withdrawal column. She wouldn't be coming back to Sweet Valley, so she might as well take it all.

A momentary pang of regret pricked her heart. It seemed ages ago that she had watched the money add up and planned to use it for college. That would never happen now.

But who cares? she thought, banishing the bittersweet nostalgia. She had new plans now. With Buzz.

She crossed the remaining distance to the tellers' line and stood to wait her turn. Minutes ticked by, and the line inched forward sluggishly. Once Molly glanced at the clock, concerned about being late. Then she laughed silently. Being late for class was pretty insignificant now, considering that she was running away.

Buzz's words came back to her, fuzzy and faraway as they had been when she heard them the night before. "Nobody understands you like I do. . . . We belong together. . . ." Much of it was still a pot-smoke blur, but one thing was clear: no one wanted her in Sweet Valley. She didn't belong there anymore. And she wondered whether she ever had.

"Next, please."

Molly stepped up to the window and pushed her passbook under the grille. The teller read the withdrawal slip and glanced at the passbook balance. "Did you want to close your account, Miss?" the woman asked.

"Well, yeah. I guess so."

The teller began pulling forms together in a small pile. "If you'll just fill—"

"I don't have a lot of time," Molly broke in hastily, annoyed at the delay. She was in no hurry to get back to school, but she couldn't stand the oppressive atmosphere of the bank much longer. "Can't I just have my money, please?"

The teller looked irritated. "If you want to close your account, you have to complete these forms. It's bank policy."

Inwardly Molly groaned. "What if I leave something in the account?"

"Well, in that case," the teller said primly, "you wouldn't be closing the account, would you?"

"Then may I have another withdrawal slip, please?" Molly tried to keep her growing feeling of panic under control. The line behind her was growing longer, and she saw people look impatiently at their watches. Molly began to feel claustrophobic and wished desperately she could get out of there.

On the fresh slip Molly scrawled $2,300 and shoved it back immediately. The teller looked as though she might have something else to say, but with a last glance at Molly's anxious face, she inserted the passbook into the machine and entered the amount.

"How would you like it?"

Molly stared blankly back at her. For some reason, she couldn't make herself understand what the woman was saying. "What?"

"The money. What size bills?"

"Oh. I don't care. Fifties, I guess."

The woman received this with a startled look, but she shrugged and began counting out forty-six fifty-dollar bills.

Molly's heart sank when she saw the size of the stack, but she didn't want to wait any longer. "Thanks," she muttered, turning away. She stepped to one side and tried folding the bills to fit in her pocket.

"Molly! There you are!" The voice came from right behind her, and Molly spun around with the money fanned out in her hand.

It was Elizabeth Wakefield, and her blue-green eyes widened with surprise as she noticed the wad of money clutched in Molly's fist.

"What is it, Elizabeth?" Molly said curtly, meeting the blond girl's eyes defiantly.

Elizabeth stared at her for a moment and then seemed to remember what she was doing. "Uh, Molly, I wanted to talk to you."

Raising her eyebrows in surprise, Molly began walking away. "I don't think we have anything to talk about," she said in a cold voice.

"I think we do. Wait, Molly."

At that, Molly spun around, angry tears springing to her eyes. "Wait for *what*, Elizabeth? I've done all the waiting I'm going to do, OK? Leave me alone." Her voice rang out in the hushed bank.

Startled faces looked in their direction, and Molly found she was still clenching her money in one hand. Her face burning red, she stuffed it into two pockets and walked quickly toward the revolving doors.

But running footsteps behind her told her Elizabeth hadn't given up. *Why is she tormenting me?* Molly wondered.

"Molly! Please. We need to talk about Regina and what happened."

"Why? So you can lay the blame on me?" Molly choked, pushing blindly through the doors. "No way!"

"Molly, no! Justin and I need to talk this out with you. We all need—"

"Justin?" Molly stopped and looked searchingly into the other girl's flushed face.

Elizabeth stopped, her smile becoming eager. "Yes. I talked to him this morning and . . ."

Molly felt her face grow hard. Why was it that when Elizabeth talked to Justin he listened, but when Molly did, he bolted like a frightened rabbit? Her eyes narrowed with a rage she didn't know she could feel.

"No, thanks. I've been your scapegoat long enough, Elizabeth. So you can take your talking and shove it."

With that, she dodged into the crowd and ran down the sidewalk. Tears streamed down her cheeks, and she brushed them aside angrily. She bumped into pedestrians who shouted after her, but she ignored them. She needed to go someplace where she could think. Running blindly, she ducked into an alley and leaned back against the brick wall.

In the back of her mind was a nagging certainty that Elizabeth had sought her out in good faith, that she was trying to make amends. But Molly had chosen her path, and she couldn't bring herself to turn from it now.

"Buzz understands," she repeated mechanically. She stared at an empty gin bottle lying in the gutter. "I don't care what Elizabeth says. I'm leaving, and that's final. No one can stop me."

Justin made his way slowly through the stream of students pouring out of the cafeteria at the end of lunch. It seemed fitting to him, when he considered it in his usual ironic way. He was always going against the current, no matter what.

Well, this time he was going to do the right

thing. After Elizabeth had left him in the library, he had done a lot of thinking—about himself, and about Molly.

He knew now that he had given up on her too easily. Their friendship had been worth fighting for, only he had been too caught up in himself to realize it at the time.

Even when he was getting to know Regina, there had been something holding him back. Regina guessed what it was: Molly. Molly was always in the back of his mind. He knew now he couldn't push her out of his life. It would be as futile as trying to deny a part of himself.

Ever since Regina's death, he had been using his own feelings of guilt and remorse as an excuse to shut Molly out. Well, she was no more to blame than he was, he knew now. And he had to tell her that.

He stood still in the middle of the cafeteria. Only a few scattered people remained in a far corner. The kitchen workers were already wiping off the tables.

Justin was momentarily taken aback. Somehow he couldn't take in the fact that Molly wasn't there waiting for him. He had gotten himself so psyched up to talk to her at last that he just assumed she would be there. Now he wasn't sure what to do. He stood frowning, remembering the decision he had made in the library.

As she was leaving the library, Elizabeth had said she was going to talk to Molly herself. At least he could relax about the urgency of the situation. If Elizabeth had already talked to Molly, she knew she wasn't alone anymore. He could go to her house that afternoon to tell her how sorry he was and that he wanted them to be friends once more. It would be like old times again.

Or better yet, he could cut his afternoon classes and try to find her at school. There was no reason not to find her as soon as he could. He owed her that much.

He glanced up at the clock on the wall. He knew Molly's schedule. He would cut his classes so he could be right there to meet her outside her classroom. If he went to his own classes, there was a good chance of missing her. This way, if he missed her at one, he could just wait until the next one. Sooner or later, he'd catch up with her. All he had to do was wait.

Ten minutes before the final bell, Justin was pacing nervously in the second-floor hallway. He hadn't so much as glimpsed Molly between classes after lunch, and he hadn't been able to find her in any of the places where most of the students hung out. An uneasy feeling was growing in the pit of his stomach.

He glanced at the door of room 211. It was possible he had missed her, and she had already gone in to her American history class before he found her. Digging his fists deep into his pockets, he began walking again.

"*Mister* Belson. May I ask what you are doing, strolling around up here?"

With an inward groan, Justin turned to face Mr. Cooper, the school principal.

"Do you have a class this period, Justin?"

"Yes, but I—"

"But you have an explanation, right?" Mr. Cooper rocked back and forth on his heels, hooked his thumbs in his vest pockets, and pursed his mouth. "Justin, Justin," he said with weary patience. "When are you going to shape up? Tell me that."

Justin opened his mouth and shut it again without speaking. How could he explain about Molly? There was no way the principal would ever understand. Besides, "Chrome Dome," as they called the bald-headed principal, didn't have much sympathy for Molly anyway. Justin watched in helpless silence as Mr. Cooper pulled a pad of detention slips from his suitcoat pocket.

"I have the distinct honor of hosting detention this afternoon," the principal went on. "And I'm really looking forward to seeing you there."

His eyes grew hard as he emphasized the last few words.

At that moment the bell clanged, and Justin's eyes flew to the door of room 211. If Mr. Cooper wanted to say anything more, he was just going to have to wait. Doors opened all around them, and students began milling out into the hallway, talking in animated voices.

"Justin," Mr. Cooper said impatiently. "I'm not through with you yet."

Justin ignored him, his eyes riveted on the one open door that concerned him. There was no sign of Molly.

Suddenly he caught sight of Elizabeth coming down the hall toward him, and their eyes met. Elizabeth opened her mouth to speak, and Justin sensed she had something important to tell him. But Jessica ran up and caught her by the arm, and Mr. Cooper grabbed Justin's shoulder.

"Now you listen to me, young man. I've had just about enough of you and your slack attitude. Have you forgotten that you're on academic probation? It doesn't seem to mean very much to you, does it? But if you keep this up, I'm going to bust your tail right out of this school. Maybe that would get through your thick skull."

Justin glanced his eyes away from Elizabeth and back to Mr. Cooper's furious red face.

"Sorry," he mumbled. "It won't happen again." He took the detention slip Mr. Cooper was holding out and stuffed it into his pocket. Right now he would say anything just to get away. He had to catch up with Elizabeth and find out what she had been trying to tell him. It had to be about Molly.

"And another thing . . ." the older man went on, his voice droning on into a mere buzz of sound in the noisy hallway.

Frantically Justin watched as Elizabeth disappeared down the corridor, led firmly by Jessica, who was talking nonstop and gesturing wildly with her hands. She turned once and gave him a pleading look. Then she shook her head sadly. Justin felt his heart pounding in his chest. Something was wrong. Definitely wrong.

"So why don't you just come with me now, Mr. Belson," Mr. Cooper's voice faded in again, and Justin turned around with a jerk. The principal took him firmly by the arm. Until four-thirty, when detention was over, he wouldn't have a chance to find out what had happened between Elizabeth and Molly. Until then he was virtually a prisoner.

Ten

Elizabeth pushed open the door to the newspaper office, and Jessica followed her in, still chattering excitedly about her ideas for the scholarship fund.

"So that's the angle I really think we should take," Jessica finished, tossing her pink duffel bag onto a table. She looked around speculatively as Elizabeth put her books neatly on a shelf. "Boy, this place is a dump."

"You're one to talk," Elizabeth said affectionately. Jessica wasn't known for her orderliness, but criticizing *The Oracle* was second nature to her. Jessica liked having a sister who was well known as a writer; but she couldn't understand *anyone* spending *so* much time cooped up inside with a typewriter when there were so many more interesting things to do.

Elizabeth's eyes traveled around the cluttered room, coming to rest on the photo-covered bulletin board, the beat-up filing cabinets, and the overstuffed bookcases. That room had been the site of many happy, contented hours in Elizabeth's life. And in times of emotional conflict, it could be a true refuge, as she had discovered on many occasions. Coping with Regina's death was somehow easier in that room with the old typewriters and familiar clippings scattered around. Maybe Jessica couldn't understand it, but Elizabeth loved that office.

"Which is your typewriter, Liz? This one, right?" Jessica yanked the dustcover off the typewriter that Elizabeth always used and pulled out the chair. "Come on. I want to get out of here by dinnertime if it's possible."

"All right, all right." Elizabeth sighed and took her place behind the typewriter. But she couldn't focus on the article Jessica wanted her to write. Her mind kept straying back to Molly and the desperate look Justin had thrown her in the hallway. It was probably just her imagination that read such significance into the scene at the bank, she told herself firmly. Besides, it was none of her business if Molly Hecht wanted to take a lot of money out of her account. If she was going to get any work done, she just had to put the two out of her mind and concentrate.

As she reached for a sheet of typing paper, the door swung open and Olivia Davidson came in, followed by Penny Ayala, editor of *The Oracle*. Both girls had their hands full of file folders, and Penny was also holding a sheaf of galley proofs from the printer.

"Hi, Liz. Hi, Jessica," Penny said, dumping her load with a sigh of relief. "Over there is fine," she added to Olivia, the arts editor of the paper.

"What brings you here, Jessica?" Olivia asked as she stacked the manila folders on top of a filing cabinet. "I didn't think the newspaper office held many charms for you."

"Well, generally it doesn't," Jessica said with a snort, hitching herself up onto the table. "But Liz and I are writing an article about the scholarship fund for the next edition. So, *voilà*."

Olivia smiled and sat down with them. "That's one story that didn't wait for the newspaper. The whole school knew about it by yesterday afternoon." Her expression was thoughtful as she toyed with a blue editing pencil. Since she was the steady girlfriend of Roger Barrett Patman, Bruce Patman's cousin, she had spent a lot of time with Regina up at the Patman estate. Sensitive, artistic, and caring, she had had a lot

121

in common with the beautiful Regina, and Elizabeth knew she was feeling her friend's loss deeply.

"Well, rumors aren't the same as facts," Penny reminded them, pushing her short, blunt-cut hair behind her ears. The editor-in-chief pulled out a chair to join them at the big table. "So make sure you explain it as fully as possible so nobody has the wrong idea about it."

"Yessir," Elizabeth chuckled and gave Penny a sharp salute. She rolled paper into the typewriter, then began to peck out a few words, biting her lip as she concentrated. She had already given the story a great deal of thought and knew pretty well what she was going to write, regardless of her twin's suggestions.

"All right, Jess," she said, her fingers gaining speed as they moved over the keys. "I'm just going to rough out a first draft, and you can tell me what you like and what you want to take out or change."

Penny and Olivia leaned over to watch, too, as the article took shape under Elizabeth's hands.

Jessica Wakefield, president of the Pi Beta Alpha sorority, has announced a plan to raise college scholarship money as a memorial tribute to Regina Morrow, whose tragic death has deeply touched us all here at Sweet Valley High.

The fund, which will be administered by an executive committee of students and faculty, will award grants every year to a deserving college-bound senior, starting next year.

Jessica said that candidates for the award should have demonstrated courage in the face of adversity or have overcome a personal handicap or obstacle. In this way, the fund will commemorate Regina's inspiring triumph over deafness.

At this time, it is planned that candidates will be nominated, either by a teacher or a fellow student. The executive committee will then review the applicants and select the one who best fulfills the qualifications described above.

The sorority will kick off the fund drive in a few weeks with a dance marathon, and the entire school is invited to help raise money. Jessica stressed that Pi Beta Alpha only initiated the scholarship fund and does not want to exclude anyone from helping who cared about Regina. All donations and suggestions for fund-raising will be gratefully received.

It is also hoped that with this tribute to Regina, the cause of her tragic death will remain firmly etched in our memories. If

her loss inspires students here at Sweet
Valley High to say no to drugs, then Regina will not have died in vain.

There was silence as the four girls finished
reading Elizabeth's article. For a moment none
of them spoke. Then Jessica cleared her throat.
"That's fine, Liz. I don't think you need to
change anything."

Elizabeth noticed Penny restraining a grin.
"It *is* good, Liz," Penny said as her eyes scanned
the story again. "We'll run it on page one."

Reaching out to touch Jessica's hand, Olivia
said softly, "Thanks for coming up with the
idea, Jessica. It was a really great thing to do."

"Well, this is a pretty solemn bunch."

The rich, deep voice came from the open
door, and the four girls turned to see Mr. Roger
Collins, the newspaper adviser, walk in.

He set his knapsack on a chair and gave them
all a disarming smile. With his strawberry-blond
hair, rugged jaw, and twinkling blue eyes, most
girls at Sweet Valley High thought he looked
like a younger Robert Redford. And he had a
personality to match his good looks, too. Friendly,
dedicated but demanding, and open-minded,
Roger Collins ranked among the most popular
teachers at the school.

Elizabeth returned his grin. "I'm working on

an article about the scholarship fund," she told him. Catching a meaningful look from her twin, she added quickly, "I mean, Jessica is really doing most of the work. I just put her thoughts into my own words."

"Oh, really? I didn't know you were interested in writing too, Jessica," he said as he came to join them at the table. His blue eyes crinkled at the corners as he smiled down at her. "I guess it runs in the family."

Tossing her honey-gold hair back, Jessica said, "I guess so. Liz is really helping out, though."

He nodded gravely and gave Elizabeth a knowing look. "Well, let's see this piece of journalistic excellence." Reaching across Elizabeth's typewriter, he pulled the paper out with a snap.

Elizabeth watched nervously as her favorite teacher read her article. Even after months of writing features and the weekly "Eyes and Ears" gossip column, she still felt that flutter of anxiety in her stomach when her work came under Mr. Collins's close scrutiny. He was a tough critic but a fair one, and Elizabeth valued his opinion.

When he finished reading, he looked up to meet her apprehensive eyes and broke into a wide smile. "Very nice, Liz—and Jessica," he added. "Very nice. It's a good, strong ending."

Olivia's expression was thoughtful. "I hope

you're right about it, Liz. I mean, I hope this does make people think twice before they try drugs."

"I always wonder why people do it, you know?" Penny added. She leaned forward on her elbows. "I mean, I know there are a lot of troubled kids out there, but why drugs? They must know it's a dead end. There's more than enough information around about how dangerous they are."

"I still think it's all Molly Hecht's fault." Jessica sat back in her chair and crossed her arms. "No matter what anyone says—"

"Lay off Molly," Elizabeth cut in softly.

Jessica stared at her, and the others turned to look at her.

"What is it with you and Molly all of a sudden?" Jessica asked. "You've really been sticking up for her for some bizarre reason."

"Your sister is right," Mr. Collins said. He rubbed his chin thoughtfully as he looked at Jessica's stormy face. "Maybe in some ways Molly has some responsibility—even though ultimately, it was Regina's choice," he added quickly.

He nodded, as if to himself, and went on. "Maybe we all have some responsibility—to make sure our friends are all right, to keep an eye out for trouble. But think about the way people in this school have been treating Molly Hecht. She's not having a particularly easy time right now."

There was an uncomfortable silence at the table, and Olivia drew a deep breath. "I—I guess it just helps ease the pain to take it out on someone," she said hesitantly. Blushing, she looked down at the table.

"Yes, it helps *your* pain," agreed Mr. Collins. "But what about Molly's pain? Did you ever consider that she had feelings, too? And that she feels as much grief as the rest of you—and maybe even more?"

Elizabeth cast a quick look at her twin. It hurt her sometimes that her sister could be insensitive to other people. And it hurt that she hadn't been able to make Jessica understand. But perhaps Mr. Collins could get through to her.

"She's a really messed-up kid," Jessica said feebly, not meeting her teacher's eyes. "She's into drugs."

"And maybe there's some underlying pain that drove her there. And she's not going to be able to get out of that trap if you all keep pushing her back in."

With some hesitation, Elizabeth decided to tell them what Nicholas had confided in her that morning. "I think you should know that Molly went to Regina's grave yesterday. I—I think it was because no one else would listen to

her. She does need help. Mr. Collins is right."
Her voice sank to a whisper as she finished,
and a fresh wave of guilt swept over her as she
recalled her own treatment of Molly.

The others were silent as they took in her
story. Then Penny tapped her pencil against
the table and nodded. "I think there's another
newspaper story in this," she said briskly. "I
think we should make a point of saying that
we're all responsible for helping people out of
trouble. It's no good just screaming about how
bad drugs are. If we don't do something to help
someone who's using them, there isn't much
point."

"Good, Pen," Mr. Collins said and gave her
an encouraging wink. "Let's run that story next
to Liz's."

"But Molly—" began Jessica, obviously troubled by her own thoughts.

Elizabeth put her hand on her twin's arm.
"Molly needs help, not hate, Jess. That's what
I've been trying to tell you. Just try to see it her
way."

For another long moment, Jessica frowned at
her sister. Elizabeth could tell her twin didn't
want to admit the situation wasn't as simple as
black and white, good and bad. But finally,
Jessica looked down at the tabletop and sighed
heavily. "I guess . . . I think I know what you

mean now." She shook her head. "Molly must feel awful."

Mr. Collins stood and rested his hand briefly on Jessica's shoulder. "Then you've come a long way toward understanding, Jessica. A lot of people never get that far. So try to keep it in mind, will you?"

Jessica looked up at Mr. Collins. "Yeah. I will."

"Now let's get this newspaper put together, girls. What do you say?"

A tremendous feeling of renewal, like sun after a rainstorm, spread throughout the room. They all stood up, ready to go on. Penny grabbed several pages of galleys and a blue pencil and nodded at Elizabeth. "You've got a column to write now, don't you?"

Elizabeth breathed a sigh of relief and smiled tiredly at her editor. "Yeah. I guess I do." But even as she turned back to the typewriter, the vague sense of worry came creeping back. They may have overcome a big hurdle in the newspaper office, but Molly was still out there on her own.

Eleven

Justin looked down at his mother as she lay sleeping on the couch. His heart full, he tucked a light blanket around her gently so as not to wake her up. But she didn't stir. She slept the heavy, dreamless sleep of a person on tranquilizers. He clenched his jaw and turned away to turn off the TV she had fallen asleep watching.

It was time he did something about her, he told himself. It was no use pretending there was nothing he could do about her dependence on sedatives. There were no excuses. For anything. Whatever her faults might be, *his* biggest fault was not trying to help her before now.

Out in the kitchen, he fixed himself a meager dinner of a cheese sandwich and a glass of orange juice. He didn't have much of an appetite, though, and his eyes kept darting to the digital clock on the counter. It was seven o'clock, and he felt frustrated that there was nothing he could do at that moment. About his mother. About Molly. About any of the problems that were crowding up his life.

His mind went back to the scene at Molly's house, where he had gone as soon as detention was over. Mrs. Hecht met him at the door and refused to let him see Molly.

"She's grounded and can't have any visitors," she told him coldly, eyeing him with obvious suspicion from the half-open door.

"But it's really important, Mrs. Hecht," he pleaded with her, trying to keep his voice even. He knew she didn't like him and thought he was responsible for the trouble Molly was in. He couldn't make her understand how urgent it was that he talk to Molly. He knew he could stand there explaining all night long and she wouldn't hear a thing he said.

"It can wait till school tomorrow, Justin. You can't talk to her now, and you can't call her on the phone. And that's final." It was final, because she slammed the door in his face.

Justin chewed a mouthful of his sandwich, forcing himself to swallow in spite of his sick feeling. Then he washed it down with a gulp of juice and regarded the telephone with an angry scowl. There was a chance Molly might answer the phone if he called. Just as he reached his hand toward the receiver, the telephone rang shrilly, breaking the silence of the quiet house. He jerked his hand back in surprise before picking it up.

"Hello?" he muttered. His apprehensive feeling intensified.

"Justin? This is Liz Wakefield. I think something might be wrong."

His heart began pounding in his ears. "What do you mean?" He couldn't believe his voice sounded so normal.

"I should have told you before, but I tried to tell myself it didn't mean anything. I've had this terrible feeling all afternoon and now—" He heard her draw a quick breath before going on. "I followed Molly to the bank this afternoon during lunch, and she had taken out a lot of money—a lot," she repeated ominously. "I just felt I had to tell you. Do you think she might be—I don't know—planning something drastic?"

Running away. She's running away. Justin knew it as certainly as if Molly had told him herself. He closed his eyes and made himself stay calm. He had to stay calm for Molly's sake.

"Do you think maybe we should go talk to

her?" Elizabeth asked, her voice hesitant. "I didn't have much luck getting through to her before."

He made a quick decision. "I'll come pick you up, Liz."

"Great," she said, then gave him her address. "I'll be ready whenever you get here."

Only pausing long enough to scrawl a quick note to his mother in case she woke up, Justin grabbed his jacket and ran out to the car. Within minutes he was turning up the quiet, tree-lined street where the Wakefields lived. As soon as he had pulled up to the curb, Elizabeth came running down to the street from her house, shrugging into a sweater as she ran.

She darted a quick look at him and got in without speaking. Nodding briefly, he pulled away, made a U-turn, and headed the car across town. They were silent as they made for Redwood Drive, and Justin prayed fervently they wouldn't pass any patrol cars on the way: the speedometer read sixty-five.

"I stopped by Molly's house this afternoon," he said in a low voice as he pulled onto the winding road where the Hechts lived and eased up on the gas pedal. "Her mom wouldn't let me in, but now I'm not leaving until I've seen Molly." He negotiated a sharp turn.

"*Stop!*" Elizabeth put a hand on his arm, and he pulled over, staring at her in surprise. She

134

nodded her head in the direction they were headed. "Look."

Up the road, in the twilight, he could just make out Molly stepping into the driver's side of her mother's car, a bulging knapsack over her arm. The car pulled onto the road and glided past them.

Without a word, Justin backed into a driveway and turned back down the way they had come, keeping the red car in sight.

"I don't like this," Elizabeth muttered, frowning ahead into the dim light.

"Me, either. Let's just see where she's headed, and then we'll know what's going on."

They followed the car as it turned into the state highway without slowing down. The tires of Justin's car screeched in objection as he tried to keep the other car in sight. His hands gripped the steering wheel, and his eyes were glued to the taillights of the car in front of them. *Molly, what are you doing?* he cried out silently. *Whatever it is, don't do it!*

"I can't believe it's gone this far," Elizabeth said in a low, intense voice. "She's just got to listen to you, Justin. She has to."

Justin said nothing but kept his eyes fixed straight ahead.

"They turned off up ahead," Elizabeth observed moments later as the red car signaled for a right and disappeared. Then she drew in her breath. "It's Kelly's."

He nodded grimly and pulled into the parking lot just in time to see Molly threading her way among the parked cars. As he was about to open his door and call out to her, he saw a man step out of the shadows behind the building. Instantly, Justin recognized the lithe build and longish, dark hair. It was Buzz.

"Get to the phone and call the cops," he said tersely, as Molly and Buzz began talking. They seemed to be having some kind of argument. Elizabeth's eyes were wide as she stared back at him. "It's Buzz," he explained. "The guy the police are after for dealing drugs."

She nodded quickly and opened the passenger-side door. Then she leaned back inside. "What are you going to do?" she asked.

"I'm going to follow them—try to head them off if I can. But it's a safe bet they're heading out of town."

"Which way?"

Vital seconds ticked by as he tried to deduce which way a fugitive like Buzz might bolt. *If I were him, where would I feel safe?*

"South," he said, praying his instincts were right. "Get the cops out to old route seven. They'll go that way 'cause no one ever uses it anymore. Better hurry up."

"Right." She slammed the door and darted away toward the phone booth silhouetted under a streetlight near the road.

He followed her with his eyes and then turned back toward the shadows behind the tavern. Buzz reached out a hand to caress Molly's cheek, and Justin felt a wave of anger surge through him. He watched with increasing fury as the two climbed into an old green Camaro parked nearby and pulled out. They headed south out of town and took the turn for the old, seldom-used highway, just as Justin had guessed they would.

Shifting into gear, Justin waited for them to get ahead. Then he followed. He didn't want to give the alarm too early, since the police would need time to get into position. But he itched to slam his foot down on the gas pedal and overtake the green Camaro. He desperately wanted the satisfaction of planting his fist on Buzz's jaw. The guy had a lot to answer for. More than Regina, more than Molly: Buzz had to answer for messing up a lot of lives.

As his anger at Buzz mounted, Justin drove his car closer and closer without realizing it, until he was only a few car lengths away. He could see Molly's profile clearly as she turned to speak to Buzz, and Justin found himself pleading with her under his breath.

"Molly. Molly, come back. Don't do it! Don't do this to yourself."

Almost as if she heard him, she turned and looked out the rear window. There was obviously enough light for her to see him by, or at least make out his car, because the shock of recognition registered on her face for an instant. She turned to Buzz again and pointed. He looked quickly over his shoulder. Instantly the Camaro surged ahead.

"OK, man. That's it. You asked for it," Justin growled, pressing his foot down in response. The road sped by under his wheels, and the two cars barreled down the deserted rural highway at seventy miles per hour. Justin's eyes were narrowed with concentration as he held his car steady, and he darted quick, analytical looks up ahead to scout out the lay of the land. A wide curve was approaching.

"It's now or never," he whispered. Holding his breath, he floored it.

His car leaped forward at his touch. He overtook Buzz and Molly on the inside of the turn and then stuck to the middle of the road, easing his foot up slightly. Honking wildly, the other car tried to pass, first on one side and then the other. But Justin kept cutting them off. When both cars were down to a safer speed, he held his breath and slammed on the brakes.

A squeal of tires behind him told him his trick had worked. The Camaro swerved into the scrubby grass at the side of the road and rolled to a stop. Without waiting, Justin jumped out of his car and raced toward Molly.

"What the hell do you think you're doing, man? Are you crazy?" Buzz screamed at him as he yanked open his door.

Molly's face was deadly white as she opened her door and stepped out, and her legs were trembling. "What are you doing, Justin? Get out of here! I don't want you!"

"Molly, don't go."

Their eyes locked, and Justin stood in a silent agony of anticipation, his chest heaving. Molly's lips opened, and she shook her head.

"Get your car out of the way, man," Buzz cut in sharply, coming to Molly's side. "And leave her alone. She doesn't want you, you heard her."

"I'm not leaving."

Visibly twitching with nerves, Buzz glanced back down the road in the fading light. Justin suspected, in some remote corner of his mind, that the guy was on cocaine. But he never took his eyes off Molly.

"Don't go," he repeated, taking a step toward her.

She backed up instantly. "It's none of your business," she said shakily. "It's my decision."

"That's right," Justin agreed, taking another step forward. "Just like it was Regina's decision to do those lines of coke. But somebody should have stopped her, and I'm stopping you."

"You can't do this to me!" she wailed, raising her hands to cover her ears and squeezing her eyes shut. "You can't do this to me!" Her voice cracked with pain, and she began to shake uncontrollably with the built-up tension of the last two weeks.

With a grunt of irritation, Buzz reached for Molly's arm and yanked her around to face him. "Come on, Molly," he said, shaking her roughly. "We're getting out of here. We agreed. Now tell your pal here to move his heap out of the road."

"Molly, don't throw your life away like this! He's not worth it!"

"Come on, Molly! Let's get out of here."

Justin took her other arm, willing her to feel what he was trying to tell her. "Don't let Regina have died for nothing!" he gasped hoarsely, filled with guilt for the pain he was obviously causing Molly. Her whole body was shaking. "Don't let him ruin your life, too!"

"Get out of here, man. She's going with me!"

Buzz shoved Justin away and dragged Molly backward toward the car at the side of the road.

Finally she broke. "Stop it! Stop it," she screamed, bursting into sobs. She wrenched her arm away from Buzz and ran back onto the pavement.

Justin stared at her, feeling tears spring to his own eyes. "Molly. Molly, I need you. Please don't leave me. I feel so alone."

With another heart-wrenching sob, she stumbled forward into his arms and clung to him. Buzz swore fiercely and darted across to them.

"Give me the money, then," he demanded, grabbing for Molly's shoulder bag.

"Get out of here, you creep! Just get away!" Justin shouted, pushing away Buzz's hand. "You've already done enough damage. So just get lost."

There was a look of sheer desperation in Buzz's eyes. "I need that money, man. And you're not stopping me." He made a swift movement as he backed up a step, and Justin saw the glint of sharp steel in the fading light.

Molly pulled her head up then and gasped. "He's got a knife, Justin!"

With a rough shove, Justin pushed Molly away from him and faced the drug dealer, keeping his eyes locked with Buzz's. The knife sliced tentatively through the air between them, as Buzz passed it back and forth between his hands.

Then he sprang forward, and Justin side-stepped him. Buzz swore and lunged again as Justin leaped to his right. An atmosphere of suspended reality seemed to surround them, as if time had stopped and this deadly serious showdown wasn't really taking place at all. But Justin knew that it was. They were standing in the middle of old route seven, night was falling, and this man was going to try to kill him if he could.

His long, thin legs were tensed like springs beneath him, and Justin could feel his heart pounding as adrenaline coursed through his veins. He knew Buzz was high on something, and he just prayed that would make Buzz's reflexes slower than normal. But he didn't know how much experience Buzz had at this kind of thing. All Justin knew was that he didn't have any, and he wasn't going to get a second chance if he messed up this time.

Keeping his eyes fixed on Buzz, he darted sideways and reached for a long stick he had noticed in the corner of his vision. It was pitifully thin, and he didn't think it would do much good, but it was some kind of weapon, and he waved it cautiously in front of him, ready to fend off the sharp, gleaming blade.

"You're really asking for it," Buzz growled, bending forward in readiness. "You're really asking for it, you punk."

The he sprang, knife outstretched, and Justin made a desperate, slashing swing with his stick. It cracked in two on contact with the sharp knife, but the momentum knocked Buzz to the side, and he stumbled clumsily past Justin. Without waiting to think, Justin brought his foot up as hard as he could and kicked Buzz squarely on the wrist. The knife whistled over their heads and landed with a soft click in the dust.

Astonished, Buzz met Justin's eyes again. Then Justin lunged, grabbing Buzz around the waist and bringing him down onto the road with a thud. They rolled wildly across the pavement into the grass, pummeling each other with their fists. Buzz's fingers stabbed upward toward Justin's eyes, and Justin flung himself back out of the way. Buzz scrambled to his feet, but Justin tackled him again, and they both went sprawling. Then, with a well-aimed punch, Justin cracked Buzz on the jaw. The drug pusher went limp.

Gasping for breath, Justin heaved himself to his feet and stood where he was, leaning his hands on his knees. Then he looked up to meet Molly's frightened gaze. She nodded slowly and closed her eyes.

In the distance the wail of a police siren sounded through the darkening night.

"We're going to be OK, Mol," Justin assured her, breathing painfully. He glanced down at the motionless figure on the ground and felt slightly sick to his stomach. "It's going to be all right. It's over now."

Molly stumbled forward and fell into his arms. They stood silently, their arms around each other, as they waited for the police to arrive. The nightmare was over.

Twelve

Elizabeth was putting the finishing touches on her weekly column the next afternoon when Molly Hecht put her head in the door of the newspaper office. There was a look of uncertainty on her face that changed to relief when Elizabeth smiled at her.

"Hi, Molly. Come on in." She stood up from her typewriter and hurried forward.

Molly stepped inside the office and closed the door carefully behind her. The two girls stood looking at each other in silence for a moment.

"I—I didn't really have a chance to say anything last night," Molly began awkwardly. She meandered to the table and picked up a pencil, drumming it nervously against her palm. "I just wanted to tell you that I'm sorry I acted—you know."

Elizabeth shook her head. "You don't have to apologize, Molly. We've all been acting a little crazy recently. I'm just glad everything turned out all right."

When Elizabeth had arrived on the scene with Jeffrey, who had raced over to pick her up, the police were just taking Buzz away in a squad car. Then there had been a barrage of questions fired at Molly and Justin, and they were both so shaken they could hardly answer. Seeing how emotionally exhausted Molly was, Elizabeth had taken the girl to Jeffrey's car and sat with her in the backseat, lending what silent comfort she could.

Now Molly was looking somewhat recovered from her ordeal. And more than that: the haunted look had disappeared from her eyes.

"And I wanted to tell you," Molly went on, a glimmer of a smile lighting up her face. "I'm really turning over a new leaf. No more dope, no more cutting school. My life's been a mess lately, and I really want to change it."

A huge smile spread over Elizabeth's face, and she touched Molly's arm briefly. "That's great. Really."

Shyly Molly returned the smile and then

146

looked away. "Justin says you talked him into . . . you convinced him that I was—"

"Forget it," Elizabeth broke in, waving aside Molly's embarrassment. "He was halfway there himself. I could tell he was really worried about you. He still loves you, Molly, and he just needed some encouragement, that's all."

"Yeah. Well, thanks."

A peaceful silence descended on the two girls for a moment, and Molly wandered around the newspaper office, running her hand lightly across the typewriters and bookshelves. Elizabeth sat down, resting her chin in her hands as she watched the other girl.

"It's kind of nice in here," Molly said finally when she turned to face Elizabeth. Her smile was tinged with regret. "You know, mellow, sort of."

"I know. That's why I come here, I guess." Elizabeth nodded at a chair, and Molly sat down, seeming slightly ill at ease, as though she still had something she needed to say.

She gave a tiny shrug. "Maybe I could—I don't know, do a story sometime."

"That'd be great. Anytime you want."

Suddenly Molly chuckled and leaned back against her chair. "This is so weird. I mean, I wasn't always so messed up, but I was never really into school or anything. Now I kind of want to be."

Smiling, Elizabeth nodded and let Molly ramble on.

"And Mr. Collins is going to talk to my parents, too," Molly continued, looking down at her hands. "He said he'd try to make them understand, and go a little easier on me. He said something about some kind of counseling group or something."

Elizabeth shook her head in amazement. "He's really a good guy. But he must really believe in you, too, if he's willing to help you."

Molly's eyes rose to meet hers, and a faint blush stole over Molly's cheeks as she looked away again. "He also said he'd—he'd nominate me for the scholarship next year if I really pull myself together. But I told him I had to ask you and the Morrows if"—she swallowed, and moved her shoulders awkwardly—"if it's OK."

"Oh, Molly, no—you don't have to ask," Elizabeth protested, vigorously shaking her head. "If you earn it, you deserve it, no matter what. You don't need anybody's approval for that."

"I know. It's just that—"

"Look." Elizabeth laid a hand on Molly's arm and met her eyes squarely. "If you do straighten out your life and stay away from drugs, that would make the Morrows very happy. I know it would. It would make them feel that something good had come out of all this. And that would be a real gift to them."

Molly swallowed and looked searchingly into Elizabeth's face. "You really think so?"

With a heartfelt smile, Elizabeth nodded. "I know so. And I think with a little help—from Justin—you can make it, too. You're going to be the first one to win that scholarship, Molly. I can feel it."

A moment of true friendship passed between the two girls, and Molly smiled gratefully. "I'll make sure you're right, Elizabeth. I mean it."

As Elizabeth opened her mouth to speak, the door opened, and Jessica poked her head in. "Liz—oh, hi, Molly," she mumbled, flushing slightly. It was still hard for Jessica to remember that Molly wasn't the evil villain she once thought. "How's it going? Listen, Liz, I'm on my way to cheerleading practice. Can you pick me up at the front steps at four-thirty?"

"Sure, Jess. I'll see you then."

"Great. 'Bye." With a last speculative look at Molly, Jessica closed the door on the *Oracle* office and trotted off down the hall, swinging her duffel bag over her shoulder.

Being co-captain of the varsity cheering squad was one of Jessica's greatest achievements, in her opinion. Few things were as exciting as walking out in front of the roaring crowds and knowing all eyes were on her as she led the team through their paces. And it was a good team, too, she had to admit. Everyone on it had been carefully selected, and they formed a tightly knit group.

And today was a special practice, because they were going to discuss ways for the cheerleading squad to raise money for the scholarship fund. In the local paper she had seen a notice for an all-state cheerleading competition with prize money, and she couldn't wait to tell the rest of the girls on the team.

"Jess, wait up!"

She turned around and saw Cara running to catch up to her. "Hi, Cara." Cara fell into step beside her, and as they walked out the front door to the playing fields, they chatted about a new routine they were going to try later.

Just as they rounded the corner of the gym, Cara grabbed Jessica's arm. "Oh, no! I left something in my locker. Come back with me. It'll just take a second."

Rolling her eyes, Jessica nodded. "Oh, all right. I guess it doesn't matter if we're two seconds late." Being late never mattered to Jessica, because as far as she was concerned, nothing ever got started until she arrived anyway.

They slipped in through a side door and

started up a short flight of steps. Up ahead, a couple was visible silhouetted against a window. They were holding hands and talking earnestly. Jessica didn't pay much attention to them, and they didn't seem to notice her and Cara, either.

Cara put her hand on Jessica's arm to stop her. "Come on," she whispered, pulling Jessica back down the stairs.

"What? What's wrong?" Jessica demanded as they left the building and stepped outside.

"Didn't you see who that was?" Cara's eyes were wide with surprise.

Jessica shook her head. "No."

"Sandy—*and Manuel*."

"No!" Jessica looked back at the door they had just passed through. "Are you sure?"

"Positive. And what's more, I asked Jeannie this morning if there was anything going on between them, and she wouldn't tell me." Jeannie West was Sandy Bacon's best friend, and both girls were on the cheering squad.

They reached the playing fields to join the rest of the team. Jessica glanced quickly at Jeannie, who was warming up with the others. She dropped her duffel bag and looked around.

"Where's Sandy?" she asked innocently, keeping her eyes on Jeannie's face.

The other cheerleader's arms stopped in mid-swing. "Oh, she said she'd be a little late," she said in a casual tone that didn't deceive Jessica.

Cara and Jessica exchanged a meaningful look. If anything was going on between Sandra Bacon and Manuel Lopez, it was too hot to keep it a secret. But with parents like Sandy's, something like this could reach the proportions of Romeo and Juliet.

"Fine," Jessica said smoothly, giving Jeannie a reassuring smile. "We'll start when Sandy gets here."

Will Sandra Bacon's narrow-minded parents destroy her chance at happiness with Manuel Lopez? Find out in Sweet Valley High #42, available in January '88.

*Coming next month: the first Sweet Valley High Super Thriller, **DOUBLE JEOPARDY!** The Wakefield twins become interns at Sweet Valley's newspaper and find themselves in serious trouble when Jessica witnesses a crime. She knows she must find the murderer before she and Elizabeth are killed!*

Get Ready for a Thrilling Time in Sweet Valley®!

Watch for the very first SWEET VALLEY HIGH® SUPER THRILLER!

When the twins get part-time jobs on the Sweet Valley newspaper, they're in for some chilling turn of events. The "scoops" Jessica invents to impress a college reporter turn into the real thing when she witnesses an actual crime—but now no one will believe her! The criminal has seen her car, and now he's going after Elizabeth ... the twins have faced danger and adventure before ... but never like this!

Coming in November at bookstores everywhere!

Celebrate the Seasons
with SWEET VALLEY HIGH
Super Editions

You've been a SWEET VALLEY HIGH fan all along—hanging out with Jessica and Elizabeth and their friends at Sweet Valley High. And now the SWEET VALLEY HIGH *Super Editions* give you more of what you like best—more romance—more excitement—more real-life adventure! Whether you're bicycling up the California Coast in PERFECT SUMMER, dancing at the Sweet Valley Christmas Ball in SPECIAL CHRISTMAS, touring the South of France in SPRING BREAK, catching the rays in a MALIBU SUMMER, or skiing the snowy slopes in WINTER CARNIVAL—you know you're exactly where you want to be—with the gang from SWEET VALLEY HIGH.

SWEET VALLEY HIGH SUPER EDITIONS

☐ PERFECT SUMMER
25072/$2.95
☐ SPRING BREAK
25537/$2.95
☐ SPECIAL CHRISTMAS
25377/$2.95

☐ MALIBU SUMMER
26050/$2.95
☐ WINTER CARNIVAL
26159/$2.95
☐ SPRING FEVER
26420/$2.95

Prices and availability subject to change without notice.